SURRENDER TO THE HIGHLANDER

Terri Brisbin

🌹 MILLS & BOON®
Pure reading pleasure™

First published in Great Britain 2009
Harlequin Mills & Boon Limited,
Eton House, 18-24 Paradise Road, Richmond, Surrey TW9 1SR

© Theresa S. Brisbin 2008

ISBN: 978 0 263 86790 9

Set in Times Roman 10½ on 12¾ pt.
04-0709-70700

Printed and bound in Spain
by Litografia Rosés S.A., Barcelona

Terri Brisbin is wife to one, mother of three, and dental hygienist to hundreds when not living the life of a glamorous romance author. She was born, raised and is still living in the southern New Jersey suburbs. Terri's love of history led her to write time-travel romances and historical romances set in Scotland and England. Readers are invited to visit her website for more information at www.terribrisbin.com, or contact her at PO Box 41, Berlin, NJ 08009-0041, USA.

Recent novels by the same author:

LOVE AT FIRST STEP
  (short story in *The Christmas Visit*)
THE DUMONT BRIDE
THE NORMAN'S BRIDE
THE COUNTESS BRIDE
THE EARL'S SECRET
TAMING THE HIGHLANDER

Look for
POSSESSED BY THE HIGHLANDER
Coming September 2009

This book is dedicated to two groups of women
who have supported me in the last two years
and one special person—

First, the wonderful women in the office
of Dr Linda Graziano in Cherry Hill, New Jersey.
A caring group of professionals, they are also avid
romance readers and have been asking
for Rurik's story since they first read
TAMING THE HIGHLANDER.
Linda, Patricia, Pat, Helen, Shelley, Deb and Amy—
here he is! Enjoy! (And thanks!)

And to the warm and amazingly helpful women and
avid romance readers in the Stratford, New Jersey,
office of Dr Jerome Pietras. To all of you who helped
me ease through difficult situations and appointments,
many thanks and this one's for you, too!

And this is for Melissa Endlich, my editor,
who has been a help to me more than she will ever
know over this last year. She understood
and loved Rurik as much as I did.

Saying thank you is not nearly enough....

Chapter One

Lairig Dubh, Scotland
1356

His sword sang its death song and the sound pulsed through his soul, giving him strength and resolve. Swinging it over his head and aiming its sharpened tip down, Rurik Erengislsson allowed the Viking buried deep within him to rise as he became one, in that instant, with the messenger of death in his grip. Only his control, exerted at the last moment, kept the deathblow from being delivered to the man lying at his feet in the dirt. Raising his face to the sun, he screamed out his battle cry like a berserker of old, loud and long, until it echoed out past the buildings of the yard and even over the walls surrounding the keep of Lairig Dubh.

His opponent judiciously allowed him the moment

of triumph and did not move. The sharp tip of the sword held at Connor's neck was, no doubt, part of what held him motionless, waiting for Rurik to relent. When those watching erupted into cheering, he lifted the sword away and reached down to his vanquished foe, the man he called laird.

"I was beginning to think this was the end," Connor MacLerie, Laird MacLerie and the Earl of Douran, said under his breath. "There was an expression in your eyes I did not recognize, Rurik."

The laird brushed the dirt from him and held his hand out for his own weapon, which Rurik had tossed aside during their battle. A boy ran to pick it up and bring it back to Connor.

Rurik cleared his throat and spit in the dirt. "I do not kill those I serve."

Connor nodded at the gold armbands he now wore. The laird was an observant man. "The sword. The armbands. I suspect they are related to the visitors who stand in my hall and await your arrival there."

"Visitors?" he asked.

Nodding to another of the lads who stood watching, he leaned over and gave him instructions before handing his blade to the boy. Facing Connor once more, he knew that an attempt at feigning surprise would not be missed and would be considered an insult by the laird, who was also his friend.

"They come looking for Rurik Erengislsson. They carry word from the Orkneys…from your father."

The news was nothing he did not already know.

Two previous visits by them had not gone unnoticed, but they returned north after being unsuccessful in their quest each time. In spite of his ability to avoid them, Rurik had not been able to cast the items they sent to him away as easily as he had their written missives.

"I know," he said. Wiping the sweat from his brow, Rurik shrugged. "I do not wish to speak to them."

Connor's not-even-furtive glances over his shoulder told Rurik that the men approached from behind. Although quite capable of knocking them to the ground, he understood that Connor had welcomed them and had thus protected them with his name and hospitality. Attacking them, even if to give himself time to escape, was not possible without making the MacLerie himself an enemy. And the urge to run was growing, disconcerting him even more.

"That sword held over me in your hand tells me otherwise, Rurik." Connor clapped him on the shoulder. "You cannot run from your past forever. 'Tis a lesson I learned and one that you should consider." Leaning closer, he lowered his voice. "You need not repeat my mistakes to learn from them."

That sword had been his failing. The armbands, although appealing to him, did not carry the importance of the sword. He damned his own weakness in not simply burying it when it was delivered to him. Rurik gazed over to watch the boy following his instructions on how to clean it. Giving in to the inevitable step he must take, he nodded at Connor and turned to face the two men who had dogged his every move for more than three months.

They need not remove their hoods for him to recognize two of his boyhood friends now grown. Rurik held out his hand to each in turn. Memories flashed through his thoughts reminding him of how much trouble three boys, who were all bark and no brawn, could get into when they had too much time and not enough guidance.

"Sven. Magnus."

The hesitation lasted only a moment more, until Sven reached over and pulled him into the crushing clinch given by one friend to another. Reluctant to admit even to himself how good it felt, Rurik pulled away. Magnus's reaction should not have surprised him, but it did and he barely missed having his wits knocked out of him by the blow when it came. The silence in the yard grew as he climbed to his feet, brushed some dirt from his breeches and began to laugh.

"Connor, come and meet these two worthless…"

They both jumped him when he turned back to the laird and he continued laughing as they all hit the ground. He held his own in the battle for a few minutes and then Rurik pushed them away, ending the fight and the uncomfortable beginning between them. Connor approached then and he introduced them in the Gaelic spoken by the clan here. When the laird invited them to seek the comforts of the hall, Rurik shook his head. He did not wish to hold the coming conversation in front of those here.

Leading the two out of the yard, through the gate and toward the village, Rurik felt the knot in his gut tighten. What kind of mistake was he making in wanting to hear their message?

He'd lied to Connor and knew the truth of it in his soul—he feared the words sent by his father. He dreaded the choices he would have to make once they were spoken. Swearing not to return to the northern islands was fine when there was no invitation, but now what would he do?

Sven and Magnus did not speak on the way to the cottage Rurik maintained here in Lairig Dubh for his use. A woman from the village watched over it when he was gone and kept it clean and stocked while he was here. Rurik smiled as he thought on the other things that the lovely Daracha provided to him during his stays. His body hardened and his mouth watered in anticipation of such things happening this night after the village quieted.

Sven and Magnus would have to sleep in the keep.

He pushed the door open and let them walk in first. Leaving the door open to allow the breezes to flow through, he pulled the few stools and chair near the small table and pointed for them to sit. Going to a storage cupboard, he took out a skin of ale and three cups. Filling them, he sat and nodded at Sven, the one who would most likely deliver the message.

"We have sought you for nigh onto three months now, Rurik. Why have you avoided us?"

"I had no interest in your words or the one who sent

you," he offered, not certain he believed the excuse, but it sounded like a good one.

"And now?" Magnus asked. "Why did you want to hear it now?"

Rurik looked around the cottage and wondered himself about the reasons that drove him to avoid them for months, as they'd said, and now approach. "It was time."

Sven and Magnus snorted, almost in unison, exchanged looks and then shrugged before drinking more of their ale. The tension around them dissipated, as though now that they knew he would hear them out, they did not have to worry about his trying to leave them behind.

"He wants you to come back. He is willing to recognize you as son and heir," Sven said, not bothering with niceties.

"Heir?"

The word slipped out before Rurik could stop it. The longing tore through him and his gut tightened. Years and years of fighting it and, with one word, it won.

"He needs someone to oversee his lands in Sweden. And there's a marriage offer to be considered."

Rurik tried to fight the smile and was as successful in that battle as he had been with trying to hold back the hunger for exactly what had just been offered to him. "Marriage?"

"Come now, Rurik, you know his connections. Many would like to be linked to the son of Erengisl

Sunesson. Bastard-born or not, you are an advantage to have as husband to some nobleman's daughter."

The reference to his illegitimacy stung, but he knew the truth of Sven's words. Many alliances were made through marriage and his birth would not really be an impediment to many who craved a connection to those with political or social power, or wealth. His father had all of those.

"Will you come?" Magnus asked.

Rurik held back that part of him that wished to jump at the offer. Many here depended on him and he did not wish to disappoint them. The laird was one such person, as was their uncle, who had taken him in without question and without rancor for his beginnings. Although hesitant to reveal so much about himself, Rurik knew that he must in order to make such a decision wisely.

"I will think on it, Magnus. I need time."

Sven and Magnus exchanged another look and then both of them peered around the interior of the cottage. Their plan was obvious; their distrust or suspicion palpable. They turned back to face him.

"The laird's hospitality will be extended for you both in the hall. You will have no complaints about the amount or quality of his food or the cleanliness of his keep."

He stood and waited while Sven and Magnus finished their ale. They began the walk back with him to the keep. It did not take long before women gathered along the path near his cottage. Smiling, he nodded at them as they passed. Sven and Magnus noticed them as well.

"Stay away from the virgins. The laird will take offense if you tangle with them and leave. There are enough others," Rurik said, nodding his head in the direction of several of the women with whom he'd spent time since Nara's departure, "who are willing."

Sven and Magnus now smiled at the women as they passed, nodding to one or another. Men had needs; women filled them. And when the women were willing, pleasure followed.

"One thing you should know," Rurik said in a low voice. "They believe that all men from the north are like me, if you get my meaning."

His reputation as a lover of women, and a great one at that, had been built over the years here with the MacLeries. He had shared enough nights of wine and women with Sven and Magnus to know that they would not disgrace him or their ancient heritage when it came to their treatment of women here.

Rurik and his old friends made their way to the keep, where the laird and lady provided for their comfort, and then back to the village, where the women provided them another kind of comfort.

Five days had passed since Rurik heard his father's offer and still he had made no decision. His uncle said nothing, although Rurik was certain he'd known the topic of the message. Dougal had never once spoken of what had happened to his sister, Rurik's mother, and Rurik had never asked how much he'd known. The one thing that was certain was that Dougal had taken in and provided for the son of his sister and had been his staunchest supporter in every step he took in becoming part of the Clan MacLerie.

Now, Rurik found himself hesitant to raise the issue and he turned for counsel to his friend. After the evening meal, Rurik sought out Connor's favorite place in the keep—other than his wife's bed—and found the laird there, high on the walls, observing the comings and goings in the yard.

"So, when do you leave?" Connor asked as Rurik approached.

"I have not yet decided to answer his call."

"Rurik," Connor said, slapping him on the shoulder, "you decided as soon as the words were said. Even before," he said, nodding his head at Rurik's sword. "The moment you took that sword out of hiding and used it, the deciding was done."

"I…" Rurik began but could not continue denying it.

Connor shook his head. "There is no need to deny the truth to me. And Dougal understands as well, but does not wish to talk about it with you."

Rurik did not have words to express his surprise or his gratitude for the understanding of the two people closest to him in life. Before he could embarrass himself, Connor held out his hand. "May I see the sword?"

"I would have thought you'd seen it close enough

from the ground?" Rurik chided. Taunting was much safer than to speak of what he was feeling.

"'Twas clear to me when I looked in your eyes and realized the man standing over me holding death at my throat was not the Rurik I knew that you'd made your decision." Rurik slid the sword from the scabbard and held it out, hilt first, to Connor. "A beauty," he said in a voice filled with appreciation for the work of art that a weapon like this one could be. "Is it your father's then?"

"And his father's before him. I saw it hanging behind his chair in his hall when I was growing up. Five generations of warriors in his family have used this sword."

Connor stepped back and took a two-handed hold on the hilt, swinging the sword above and around his head. Rurik knew that the sword was perfectly balanced and as lethal as it was beautiful. He watched in silence as Connor moved through a few swing-and-thrust motions with it. Only another warrior could truly appreciate a weapon such as this and, clearly, Connor did.

"And now it is yours?" he asked.

"Aye, 'twould seem so."

"When do you depart?" Connor asked. Then he added quickly, "And have you told Jocelyn yet?"

Rurik shook his head. The lady had become a good friend, but she would not take well to the news that he was leaving. And he would miss her also.

"Coward!" Connor said, one of very few who

could accuse him of such a thing and live to tell of it. "Very well, I will tell her after you have gone."

Rurik returned the sword to its place and nodded. There was too much for any words to convey properly, so he held out his arm to Connor.

"Laird," he said, bowing his head.

"Friend," Connor replied, taking his hand and arm in a tight grasp and shaking it. "You always have a place here with the MacLeries, Rurik. Know that always."

Rurik found his throat tight as Connor released him. With a quick nod and a turn, he walked away from the laird and toward his destiny.

Chapter Two

Convent of the Blessed Virgin
Caithness, Scotland

Margriet sat on the steps leading up to the small chapel and held her hands over her ears. If another of the holy sisters began to wail, she would—God forgive her—be tempted to strangle her. Granted they were only novices and young at that, but already Sister Madeline and Sister Mary were caterwauling as loudly as she'd ever heard anyone scream. Sister Suisan had fainted again, so at least her crying had stopped.

The reverend mother, Mother Ingrid, overwhelmed at the sight of the warriors at their gates, promptly ran to the church, fell to her knees in prayer and would not respond to any questions or requests. Although Mother's manner was usually one of calm and control, Margriet guessed that when confronted with such a formidable group of outsiders anyone's calm could be disturbed. That left Margriet, as was their usual custom in recent days, in charge of the others and she was uncertain what to do.

"Lady?" a soft voice broke into her quiet cone of thoughtfulness.

Margriet looked up and realized it was Sister Sigridis and she was not whispering but shouting at her. She dropped her hands. "What is it, Sister?"

"He is calling for ye again."

"Yes, Sister. He has been doing that for two days now."

"Do ye think that mayhap ye should answer him? He sounds angrier than before."

Margriet took in a deep breath and let it out before standing. Each time the warrior yelled out her name, the youngest of the nuns began their hysterics again. Lifting her long braid and tossing it back over her shoulder, she strode off toward the main gate and... him. Tugging on the thick brown gown as she walked, she prayed he would relent this time and leave them, and her, in peace. The stubborn set of his jaw in each encounter so far told her otherwise.

Truly, if it had been in a different situation, she might find him appealing. He was certainly fit and the strength in his arms—as he banged hard enough on the wooden gate to nearly shatter it—would provide strong protection to those in his care. His head, though it appeared that his custom had been to shave it of hair, was now covered with a downy layer of

pale hair. Instead of marring or softening his appearance, it both gave him a dangerous look and made
her palms itch to touch it and test its softness. It was
the only thing soft about him for even his deep voice
made her heart pound in terror at its fierceness.

Since she was the person he sought, Margriet felt
mostly irritation at his behavior and his methods of
attempting to gain her compliance. Sister Sigridis
dropped away from her side and stood a distance
from the gate as she climbed up into the guard's
tower to look over the wall.

"I asked you to stop terrifying the good sisters, sir."

The words certainly sounded brave to her ears
and she waited for his response. Margriet took a
small step forward so she could look down at him.
The man backed away a few paces, intent on looking
up at her. With the nun's habit on her, she knew he
could glimpse only a small part of her face and not
much more. The bulky robes covered her from feet
to shoulders and the wimple and long veil covered
everything else.

"And I asked Lady Margriet to present herself for
escort home, Sister. One will surely follow the other,"
he called out to her. When he stopped shouting, his
voice could be quite pleasant…for a barbarian.

"Lady Margriet has taken vows…of silence…"
she answered, thinking it an excellent reason for not
talking to him, "and she fears for her soul if she
breaks that."

Guffaws from all the men below filled the air.

Apparently the men did not think a woman capable of silence.

"Present the girl now!" He was back to yelling and banging and she feared the gate would give way soon to his strength.

"A short respite, please, sir. Let me see if I can convince her to see you," Margriet offered.

There was a buzz of conversation below among all the men there and then an answer. "An hour, good sister. You have one hour to convince the girl to speak to me or I will burn this convent to the ground and remove her myself."

She knew for a certainty the result that would occur because of his threat and her left eye and the brow above it began to twitch in anticipation. Scrunching her eye shut, she gritted her teeth the moment it began.

Loud, hysterical screaming and wailing began in the chapel and spread out as the novices there, as well as a few of the lay women, joined in the horrible chorus. The few men who worked there, tending the fields and doing the heavy labor that women could not, looked at her nervously. They could not defend the convent against this warrior's attack. Other than a few knives and a bow and quiver of arrows for hunting, they had no weapons but for some farming tools.

Margriet climbed down quickly and waved to Sister Sigridis, who shook her head. The daft girl probably thought she meant to send her out to answer his demands. "Sister, please tell the reverend mother that I will speak to this Rurik and see if I can convince him to leave me here."

"Are ye certain, lady? He might take ye by force if ye leave the safety of the walls."

Although Sister Sigridis's intention was to offer some consolation, Margriet sensed a feeling of relief in the girl at not having to speak to the man. She did not blame the sister for not wanting to do so, but she knew now that only she could work out a compromise and end this siege before it truly started.

"I am, Sister."

Margriet lifted the habit over her head and pulled the veil and wimple free, immediately sending a rush of cool air around her. Her body did not handle heat well right now and it was a relief to remove it. Tossing her extra garments to one of the servants, she thought on how she could accomplish the task. What would make the man stop his harassment and go away?

Her only communication with her father over these long years had been in writing, so Margriet decided to prepare a missive that this warrior could take with him and deliver instead of taking her.

Entering the convent through the kitchen, she shushed and soothed all those working there. Although not a nun and not officially in charge, Margriet's strong personality and innate intelligence had made it easy to "guide" the good sisters to her way of doing things here. She found that the management of people was quite enjoyable and satisfying, and knowing she was contributing to their welfare convinced her that her presence and actions were of benefit to the religious community there. With nothing to distract her, Mother Ingrid spent more hours in prayer each day and that was something that made the woman very happy. As it did Margriet.

She opened the door to the reverend mother's chambers and searched the desk for an unused piece of vellum, or one that could be scraped and used again. Finding one, she sat and composed a letter to her father explaining how she desired to remain with the sisters in the life of a religious contemplation and prayer. Surely, he would not deny her permission to serve the Lord in such a manner?

It took nearly the full hour to complete, scraping the old ink from the vellum, carefully composing and writing her words, but once she finished and sanded the parchment, she knew it would work. Rolling it up with care, Margriet walked outside, garbed herself once more as a sister and looked around for a companion to accompany her outside the walls.

None of the sisters could be trusted to carry out her instructions in this charade, so Margriet went searching for the girl who worked in the laundry, someone who rarely spoke a word to anyone. If the warrior from the North thought Gunnar's daughter was still a girl, she would present him with a girl— one who did not speak—and she would talk for her. When the girl, Elspeth, shook her head in agreement, Margriet walked to the gate with her in tow. As she

waited for Elspeth to don the other habit she'd secured, she could hear the men on the other side.
Margriet paused only to gain the promise of a truce.

"Do you swear that you will take no action against
Lady Margriet?" she called out to them, to him.

"Sister, you would try the patience of the very
saints to whom you pray! Bring the girl out now."

Elspeth smiled at his words and Margriet suspected that others had said the same thing about her
here at the convent. Still, she needed some assurance
against their superior strength and weapons. Deciding that a man's vanity could work against him, she
tried a different approach.

"This is a house of God, sir. Surely even a mighty
warrior such as yourself would agree to a truce in the
name of the Almighty."

The rude and bitter swearing that reached her even
through the thick gates spoke of other interests he
had, but Margriet waited in silence now. After a few
minutes of fierce whispers and some laughter from
the other men out there, the leader relented.

"You have your truce, Sister. Now, bring the girl
out!"

His voice roared and she could hear the wailing
again, so she tugged the veil lower on her face and
lifted the bar from the gates. Pulling it open, she
stepped out through the narrow space and Elspeth
followed, head bowed as she'd told her to do.

"Lady Margriet?" he asked.

Stepping closer, he lifted the girl's chin to get a

better look at her face. Damn the man! Margriet feared that Elspeth would bolt, but the girl remained at her side and allowed him his scrutiny. It was when he glanced at her and then stared that Margriet felt faint.

His eyes seemed to pierce into her very soul, so strong and intense a gaze that she tried to turn away from him and failed. He searched her face as though looking for something and then let his eyes drop over her body, in spite of the bulky robes and veil. It was as though he was touching her, running his hands over her flesh, and every inch of her felt scorched by his examination. Their eyes met and the moment stretched on and on until the men behind him coughed loudly. Finally she pulled her wits about herself and cleared her throat.

"This is the Lady Margriet Gunnarsdottir, from Kirkvaw. She has prepared this letter to explain her situation to her father. If you would be good enough to deliver it to him on your return…"

Her pride in getting the whole message out was crushed when he tore open the seal she'd placed and began to read the words there. Then he laughed out loud, the sound of it echoing through the trees surrounding them and out into the forests. Finally, he passed the parchment onto the one nearest him, who read it and handed it back. This second man said nothing, but only shook his head as though in disbelief.

"Sirs, you scoff at something godly and spiritual that the lady wishes to do. Will you deliver it to Lord Gunnar?"

"Nay, Sister. To deliver that instead of his daughter will be a death sentence for all of us."

He dropped the letter to the ground and smashed it under his booted foot. Margriet gasped at such wastefulness and tried to recover it. The warrior grabbed her arm and lifted her back to standing. She looked at the rough hand holding her prisoner and then at his face. No one had touched her so, no one would dare touch her in this manner, but for these few moments she was only a sister standing in the way of his mission. He seemed to realize his inappropriate hold and let her go.

"Pardon, good sister," he said softly. "I will replace that which I have destroyed and make a generous donation to atone for my actions here. Once the lady leaves with us, of course." The smile at the end of his words in no way allayed her fears or detracted from his seriousness.

Margriet, who should have learned the hard lesson of male guile long ago, found herself fascinated by the way his firm lips curved as he smiled. The expression softened his features, but did not take away from the masculine angles and lines of his face. When he smiled more, it revealed a more attractive man than she would have thought possible from their meetings so far.

He towered over her in height and, as he stepped toward her now, she moved back. Realizing the true danger in such closeness, she reached out, took Elspeth's hand and tugged the girl inside the gates quickly before he could grab her himself. Leaning on the gates with all their weight, they lowered the bar and locked it. She only just dared to take a breath when his words, spoken quietly but far more dangerously then anything he'd said so far, reached her.

"Lady Margriet, I know not who that girl is, but if you do not present yourself to me, outside these gates, at sunrise, I will burn the convent to the ground."

"Sir…" she began, but she faltered as he interrupted.

"Do not think to play me for some fool again, lady. Be outside the gates at sunrise or there will be only ashes and wailing women left here when I tie you to my horse and drag you home to your father."

She shivered at his threat and looked at Elspeth, whose face had lost all color. Her gambit had failed. Although a stranger to her, she did not doubt his resolve in this. Without another word, she pulled Elspeth along with her as she ran to the chapel. Maybe Mother Ingrid's desire for seclusion and to pray all the time was a better plan than hers after all?

It took some time to calm down the sisters and the others there and more time to accept her fate. Part of her simply could not believe that he would take such drastic measures to force her out, but when Sister Sigridis reported that his men were collecting wood from the forest and making a huge pile, the truth seemed plain to see. After the years of comfort the good sisters had provided to her, she would not allow them to be hurt in her stead.

As she lay on her pallet that night and considered what few choices she had, Margriet knew that they would never ask her to leave or force her to, but her conscience would not let the matter get to that. Gliding her hands over her now-rounding belly, she thought that mayhap this was God's work after all. Finn had promised her marriage, but something had happened that forced him to leave before he could honor that promise. Surely if she accompanied these men to Kirkvaw, found him and revealed the truth of her condition to him, he would honor his words and their love.

Surely?

Margriet was certain that she'd just closed her eyes when she woke to someone shaking her roughly. Rubbing her eyes and praying that the sickness that plagued her mornings was gone, she sat up and met the very worried gazes of four of the sisters.

"What is wrong?" she asked, rising from the pallet and tugging on her low boots. Smoothing her sleep-snarled hair away from her face as she ran toward the doorway, she waited for one of them to explain.

The smell of burning wood told her more than words could. Margriet raced from the small chamber and ran to the gates. Knowing she could avoid fate no longer, she lifted the bar and tossed it to the ground. Although they stood watching, no one stopped her or tried to convince her to stay. The thickening smoke burned her eyes as she stepped outside and faced her adversary.

Five men stood with lit torches in their hands waiting on his order. A faint expression of success crossed his face and then he covered the space between them in a few long strides, reaching her before she could react. In his hands, he held not a torch but a length of rope and his threat echoed through her mind.

"Will you come willingly or do I tie you?"

Not a sound was made by any of those watching and no one moved as this Rurik waited for her answer. In that moment the blood of her ancestors pulsed through her veins, giving her a confidence she'd not known before.

"I am Margriet Gunnarsdottir and will come willingly if you guarantee the safety of those inside."

They both knew she had no choice, but he did the most unexpected thing then. Instead of gloating as most would in such a situation, he smiled at her and she could feel his pride in her decision. Respect filled his gaze, warming her from the inside out, and then he motioned to the men to put away the torches. As one, they bowed to her.

Margriet stood stunned for a moment, trying to sort out her feelings over their actions and, in a sudden burst, the uncomfortable feeling overwhelmed her. There was no time to warn any of them and she discovered that vomiting on a man's boots did not convey the emotion she was trying to show.

Or mayhap it did?

Chapter Three

Rurik felt a certain measure of satisfaction as he watched Margriet surrender to his demands, but that feeling dulled when faced with her next action. Aye, his quarry was run to ground and the task his father set for him—a test no doubt—would be completed in a short time. Her nervous reaction could be considered usual for one of the fairer sex. His boots had worn worse in the course of their use and he did not fret over them…well not too much. It would wash off.

The gates stood open now even if the occupants of the convent remained out of sight. One nun stood at the doorway to the small church and seemed to be their watchman—turning and whispering to those inside every time he or his men moved or spoke or grunted or spit. Sven and Magnus had caught on quickly and now gestured or spoke just to see the reaction the move brought. The nun did not realize yet that she was the object of their amusement. He should stop them, for making merry at the expense of these women of God was not something he should sanction. But, their manipulation was innocent fun and no one was harmed by it.

A strong breeze carried the nauseating smell to him and Rurik knew the vomit would be harder to remove if it dried into his boots. Looking around the small enclosed yard, he spied a well and walked to it. Since the lady gave no sign of an imminent arrival, he suspected there was time enough to see to it before they left on their journey. As he reached for the bucket, the approach of an old man surprised him.

"She hasna ridden much," the man blurted out with no warning.

Rurik continued his task, tossing the bucket down the well and pulling it up once it was filled. Tilting it, he let the water pour down his legs and boots, then he used one foot to scrub the mess off the other, continuing until most of the muck was loosened. His other purpose for not responding was that he knew his silence would spur on the old man. It was not long in coming.

"She hasna left here in the years since her da sent her here," he offered. Rurik noticed the man did not stand straight but appeared wizened with many years of life.

"What has that to do with me, old man?" he asked. Finished with removing the odorous material from his boots, he tossed the bucket where he'd found it and met the man's gaze now. "Do you think I will mistreat her?"

"The daughter of Gunnar is a prize and should be treated with respect," the man replied, rising to a height Rurik would not expect possible. "Ye will answer to me for any harm done her."

The temptation to laugh filled him, but he tempered it. Both knew the man would never be able to best him in any test of skills or strength, but Rurik respected his attempts to intimidate. More interesting, the words and fervor told Rurik much about his true opponent in this confrontation—the lady Margriet.

Rurik bowed to the man and nodded. "You have my word that no harm will befall her while in my care, old man."

He peered up at Rurik, apparently considering his pledge, and then nodded with a grunt. "Ye'll do."

With all the pride of a Highland warrior, the man reached out and offered his arm. Rurik stepped over to his and clasped arms, shaking it. "What are you called, old man? And what is your place here?"

"I am called Black Iain and I tend to the flocks."

His hair may have been black at some point in his life, but Iain would be more suitably called Gray and Balding Iain now. A commotion, beginning inside the main building and spreading to the yard, interrupted any more conversation. His hand moved to his sword as Rurik turned to face the trouble. As he watched the group of women exit from the convent, he knew a sword was not necessary for this.

The weeping crowd held at its center the woman of whom they spoke. She alone did not cry or make a sound as they moved toward him. Now though, a nun's veil covered her waist-length black hair and most of her face. Her eyes, the palest blue Rurik had seen, were luminous against her pale skin, at least the skin he could see. The nun's clothing back in place, Rurik contemplated for the first time that mayhap she had truly taken her vows.

Shaking his head at the waste of it, he whistled to his men and nodded at the gate. Ceasing their antics, Sven and Magnus crossed to the gate and gathered the rest of the men together. Finally, after days of waiting, first for her acquiescence and then for her preparations, their journey would begin. Meeting her gaze over the heads of those around them, Rurik was struck by the sudden vulnerability he spied there. While secure within the convent's safety, Margriet seemed fearless. Now, when about to enter into his care, her brave face slipped and he was certain that the others were keen to it, too.

Making his way to her, he easily pushed the others out of the way and Rurik took her arm. Guiding her toward the gate, he nearly did not notice when she planted her feet and stopped moving with him. Annoyance grew once more and he turned to face her.

"No more delays, lady," he demanded. "I thought that was clear in my instructions. An hour, no more, to finish your preparations."

"Sister," she said, her lips pursed in an enticing and yet mutinous manner, at once beguiling and infuriating him for his reaction. "You may call me 'Sister.'"

Silence reigned as everyone quieted to await his response. In spite of the habit and veil, he was still not certain of her standing, but decided to give her the benefit of his doubt. "Sister, then. There are only a few more hours of daylight and I want to take advantage of every moment." *To get you as far away from here as possible and then discover your truth.*

Her next action surprised him. She stepped toward him and leaned in closer, until he had to bow his head to hear her words. "I would beg a few more minutes to say farewell to the Reverend Mother." Margriet met his gaze and he noticed tears gathering there. "I have lived here longer than I did with my father or mother and I beg your leave to speak to her privately before departing here."

Rurik lifted his head and looked at those who stood watching. Taking a breath in and letting it out, he fought the urge to strike out needlessly. Aye, he and his men had waited for nigh to three days while the woman before him thwarted his attempts to carry out his task. Aye, he wanted to be quit of this place and be on his—their—journey north. But, from her actions thus far, Margriet demonstrated that she clearly did not want to return to her home. Or perhaps the tone of the summons from her father or some words within it were the cause of her hesitancy. Regardless, he would rather be her escort than her warden.

Rurik took a different tact—and turned towards the chapel. "I would like to speak to your reverend mother myself. Perhaps if I assured her of your safety, you would feel less concern over this parting?"

She shook her head vehemently, making the veil wobble a bit to one side. "Nay, sir. She said that you terrify her and she wishes not to speak to you directly."

"Make haste then, la...*Sister.* 'Tis long past our time to be on the road."

Not wishing to give her the complete victory, Rurik turned and strode to the gate. Crossing his arms over his chest, he met the stares of his men, daring them to utter a sound. Wise men that he knew them to be, they did not. Instead they made themselves busy with the final adjustments to the pack horses.

Wise men indeed.

In a shorter time than he thought possible, the lady approached, followed by the younger woman she'd tried to pass off as herself. A chuckle nearly forced its way free as he noticed that both still dressed in habits. Rurik stepped back and allowed them to pass, watching as his men guided and assisted them onto the horses brought for their use on the trek north.

After a few more minutes while the lady's belongings were secured to her horse, they were at last on their way.

Margriet fought the urge to look back and lost the effort. The place she'd called home and the people who had become her family when her father exiled her to

Caithness grew more and more distant. Now her battle was to keep the tears that burned her eyes and throat from falling. After a final glance and a deep breath, she turned back and aimed her gaze at the road ahead.

Slipping another of the herbs into her mouth and chewing it against her stomach's distress, she struggled to focus on her future life instead of the past. Grabbing on to the thought that this unexpected intrusion into her life might actually hasten the inevitable and that thought impossible, Margriet realized that this was the first time in so many years that she would see the world outside the convent, and see her home and the sea. The thought of crashing waves and surging water shot a burst of hope and excitement through her and she tried to smile at it. Something good would come of this chaotic beginning after all.

The sun's light penetrated the thick canopy of trees surrounding them and fell onto the damp ground in scattered shadows. Though this part of the road was not new to her, the views of it were. As each of the men leading their group passed in and out of a sunbeam, their bodies were outlined in shimmering gold. Try as she might, she also lost the battle gawking at such male beauty.

In spite of her years of living in the convent, in spite of her previous weakness and the cost of it that was still to be paid, Margriet allowed herself the pleasure of inspecting the warriors who escorted her. At least those introduced to her.

Each one was appealing in his own way, and to a man, they'd inherited the height of the Norse warriors of long ago. Magnus, with his dark hair and eyes that made him appear mysterious and nearly dangerous, except when he smiled and the illusion disappeared. Sven, the opposite in coloring, allowed his wheat-colored hair to fall freely down his back and she'd noticed that his eyes were the color of the blue sky at sunset.

The trees swayed in the wind and the light shifted to surround the leader of her escort. Rurik—he'd told her without telling her his family's or father's name. It was not an uncommon name in Kirkvaw or the Orkneys so there was no way to associate him with one family or another unless he revealed it. He resisted when she frowned at the lack of forthrightness and she let it go for the moment. Her father would send only a reputable, trustworthy man and there would be time enough while they rode north to ferry across the sea to her Orkney home to discover his connections. For now, she watched as he rode ahead of her, both guiding and guarding their traveling party.

Margriet's stomach trembled and her breath hitched as she remembered his strength and his closeness and, most especially, his green eyes that changed from the color of the leaves now surrounding them to the color of the emerald she remembered on the hilt of her father's battle sword. When the object of her reverie turned as though he'd heard her thoughts, she met that intense gaze and truly lost her breath.

Although certain only a moment had passed by as she stared at him across the distance, Margriet feared others had noticed her perusal. She forced her eyes from his and shifted on her mount. Such scrutiny of a man was unseemly for a nun and she must remember her disguise or it would be of little use and protection for her or Elspeth.

When she next dared to raise her eyes, Rurik still watched her. It was his turn to break the connection that stretched then and he said something to Magnus as he turned away. It seemed that she was the subject of whatever comment had been made, for Magnus moved his horse to the side of the path and allowed the rest to pass him by…until he reached her side.

"Sister," he began. He did not seem to trip over the word as his leader did. "Rurik asked if you are well enough to increase our pace. We have much distance to cover before the light fades."

"Well enough?"

"You were ill…before," Magnus stammered as many men did when confronted by a female and certain ailments. She sat up a bit taller on her horse and cleared her throat.

"Tell Rurik to fear not, I will keep pace with him."

Magnus smiled then, exposing a pleasing countenance of masculine angles and lines that framed a wide brow and strong chin. His eyes widened in what seemed to be merriment and then, after a brief nod, he rode back to Rurik. From the shared laughter and the glances, Margriet knew for certain that she'd done something untoward. She thought on her words, but could discern nothing amiss in them.

She would never understand them.

Of course, part of her problem was a lack of experience and a dreadful lapse in judgment during her only experience! One aspect about herself that Margriet had discovered was her ability to learn quickly in new situations and circumstances. This journey would give her the opportunity to learn about men and how they acted with each other and toward women they were supposed to respect. She already knew how they treated the common woman without protection.

When those in front of her and Elspeth, who was at her side, moved faster, Margriet urged her horse to follow the pace. Adjusting herself carefully so as to not scare her mount and not fall to the ground, she lowered her head and concentrated on staying seated. Oh, she'd ridden a horse before, but not on such a journey as this, with experienced warriors who looked, from their easy manner, as though they lived on horses.

The afternoon passed at an agonizingly slow pace and soon she held on to the reins with every bit of her strength. Surely, he did not mean this as retribution for obstructing his plans? When it seemed like several hours had passed and still they rode on, Margriet was ready to consider that Rurik would show no mercy now that she was in his control. Soon, as her body tightened with pain, she was ready to beg for that which he seemed unwilling or unable to give.

"Sir!" she implored in as loud a voice as she could manage. "Sir!"

Various voices carried her message forward until she heard his order called out. Every muscle in her back and legs screamed as she tried to straighten up on the paltry cushion that was failing miserably in its attempt to protect her bottom from the abuse of the ride. Her previous practice on the nearly lame pony at the convent could never have prepared her for riding this mount at this gait. Mopping her brow once more of the sweat that gathered there, Margriet lifted her head and watched as *he* made his way back to her side.

"I confess, sir," she began as she wiped her brow and face again with the edge of one sleeve, "I confess that I have no experience in traveling at such a pace and I beg you to allow me…us…a short respite."

If she had been looking away at that moment, Margriet would never have seen the look of triumph on his face at her words. Then a moment of confusion followed and he simply nodded. What had he thought she was ready to confess? His words clarified it for her.

"Lady," he said and then paused. Clearing his throat, he met her gaze and began anew. She could see his jaws clenching as he formulated his reply. "Sister, there is no need to beg. Simply ask for what you need and I will seek to fulfill your needs."

Her lovely mouth dropped open a bit and her pale-as-ice eyes widened at his words. Then he observed a revealing blush creep up onto her cheeks and felt his cock harden.

Sweet Freya's tits! But she was gorgeous when agitated!

He should be asking for her forgiveness but instead his body continued to react to the momentary flash in her eyes that revealed so much to him. He'd learned to read a woman's expression long ago and hers said that *Sister* Margriet had more knowledge of the arts of love than a nun should have.

He could swear that she understood all the meanings in his words, which definitely bore more than one. From the way his men shifted on their horses, trying not to look openly at either of them, he knew they had as well. Her mouth closed and she swallowed several times; his view of her lovely neck was unfortunately obscured by the religious garb she wore. Finally she pushed words out and he hoped for another confession from her lips.

"A short rest, if you please," she said. "I can no longer feel my legs, sir," she whispered so that only he could hear. Most likely, she had not noticed the other men practically falling off their mounts to listen.

Rurik surveyed their surroundings, and considered the distance traveled and still to go before they would camp for the night, and nodded. Safety was his concern, and with the loss of several hours already, he was not truly happy about stopping now. He glanced at the other young nun and noticed her pale complexion. They were not seasoned travelers at all.

He raised his arm, signaling the men to pause. He watched as several rode off ahead and behind, taking up positions meant to guard their party from any surprises approaching them on the road. Rurik slid off his horse and handed the reins to one of the other men so that he could assist the women from theirs. He reached up to lift her from her place on the horse's back when she shook her head.

One thing he'd learned early in life was that some wanted or needed to make every situation more difficult than need be and that there was no way to change their predisposition to such an attitude. Margriet—Sister Margriet—seemed one of those very people. Rurik stepped back and crossed his arms over his chest, watching her antics as she tried to dismount on her own.

'Twas clear that her legs would not obey her commands to move. She shifted on top of the horse and he allowed her to try until her actions caused her mount to sidestep nervously. Rurik stepped closer, took hold of the reins and brought the horse under control.

Gunnar's daughter had a stubborn streak. 'Twas clear from the way she struggled to move legs that were clearly not going to move on their own. Although she glanced at her companion once or twice, she would not look at him. Stubborn and prideful.

Neither attributes were what he would expect in a true woman of God. Mayhap that was why Gunnar had exiled her here…? Had he hoped the good sisters would work or pray or beat it out of her? From what he remembered of Gunnar's daughter, and it was not much due to his age and interest in the pursuit of the fairer sex at the time, her mother had died soon after her birth or the birth of a sibling, and then she was gone.

Thinking back, the struggle for control of the Orkneys exploded about that same time and, with the uncertainty of loyalties and outcomes, Gunnar had been wise to send her south. Now with Caithness awarded to a Scottish earl's control and Erengisl of Sweden firmly in place as Earl of the Orkneys, her father thought the timing good to bring her home. More likely than not, with an eye to marrying her off.

Hah! Watching her nearly topple to the ground and still not ask for help, Rurik suspected her father would be as surprised as he about Margriet's vocation to religious life. He reached out as soon as he knew she would land on her arse in the dirt and took hold of her waist. Lifting her off the horse was no more trouble for him than if he was lifting a child. *Lifting* her was not the problem.

Letting go of her became the problem when he felt the narrowness of her waist and the flare of her hips in his grasp.

No, he thought a moment later, the true trouble was when she struggled against his hold and his hands slipped up high enough to feel the weight of her breasts against them. Margriet noticed; the flaring of her pale eyes revealed it, as did the way she stilled a moment later.

The best thing—well, the most polite thing—would be to release her immediately, but in that moment he did not want to be polite. His body reacted and his blood heated and surged through him, making him want to do that which his ancestors were known for— he wanted to take and pillage.

By Odin's Seed, he understood the legends of old! His body understood them and stood ready. And when she placed her hands on his shoulders, he nearly forgot everything.

"My thanks for your assistance, sir."

Her voice broke in to the maelstrom in his head and brought a halt to his wild thoughts. It did nothing for the heat that raged in his blood.

Rurik nodded and lowered Margriet to the ground. He felt the shakiness of her stance and waited a minute more for her to steady herself. Some distance was truly needed and he turned to help the younger woman. Unfortunately Magnus robbed him of his excuse to move from Margriet's side.

Standing this close, he heard her labored breathing as she tried to take a step. Her stubbornness won out again, for she stumbled against him as her legs gave out.

"Thor's Breath, la… Sister, let me help you," he said as he grabbed her shoulders and held her still.

She lifted her head and nodded in agreement, but anger flashed in her eyes at his aid. He released her after a few minutes and placed his arm under her hand so he could walk at her side.

"My thanks, sir," she said as she lifted her hand from his a few paces later.

Rurik watched as she waddled away from him, still unsteady but moving apurpose. He turned to find the men watching him with as much interest as he watched the woman. Not a good thing.

He nodded at one of the men to follow the women as they made their way off the path, obviously in need of privacy after several hours on the road. Never one to disregard or to ignore his own weaknesses, for they could be the death of him and those to whom he pledged loyalty, he considered why he reacted this way to a nun.

First, he did not expect Gunnar's daughter to be as old as she was—from his father's missives he thought her still a young lass.

Second, he did not expect her to be a nun—for the daughter of a man held in such high esteem and with such wealth as he knew Gunnar to have was a marriage prize and not a gift to the church. The sight of her in the religious habit stunned him.

But more than that, he never expected her to be the strong, organized, willful and beautiful woman that she was. From the first moment of resistance to her eventual surrender, Margriet proved herself a proud Daughter of the North. 'Twas obvious from their initial encounter to the last order she gave before she left it, that she ruled the convent. He counted at least fifty nuns and lay people living there and, from youngest bairn to oldest man, they all appeared well-fed and kept. Not an easy task for even the most experienced of stewards, let alone a nun.

Rurik swallowed against the tightness in his throat as he realized the basis for his weakness. Although he'd met her as a nun, his body and his senses saw only the woman under the garb. And the attraction he felt and the desire that filled his blood could only be dangerous.

As his eyes sought her figure as she disappeared behind some bushes, Rurik knew this was one weakness he could not afford.

Chapter Four

Elspeth's soft snore simply reminded Margriet that she was not asleep. Turning to her side away from the woman next to her, she barely stifled a groan as the hard ground revealed another place injured by the hours on horseback. Her hip spasmed and she tried to stretch her leg to ease it. Tempted though she was to try to walk some of the cramping away, the loud snore just outside the small tent spoke of the impossibility of doing just that. When her back joined in with its own aches, Margriet decided to try.

Since the tent was meant to give them a small measure of privacy, it stood only a few feet tall and two paces wide. Trying not to disturb Elspeth, she crawled out from under the blankets they shared and shimmied to the flap of the tent. Since they slept in their clothes, dressing was not a problem, but her hair would be.

Margriet suspected that her vanity over her hair would unravel her disguise, especially since the men and their leader had seen it when she panicked and ran from the convent with it uncovered. Women taking their vows cut off their hair before donning the veils and the presence of hers raised a suspicion about her truthfulness. And that was dangerous. After she braided and wrapped her hair, she reached into her bag and took out a woolen shawl. Draping it over her head, she peeked outside.

The man guarding the tent slept so close that she would have to step over him to get out. His loud snore, now alternating with Elspeth's gentler one, covered her movements. Her back and hips and legs screamed in pain as she crept over him and took a faltering step away…and into the one called Sven. Luckily, he grabbed her hands and helped her to stand up before she landed on the ground.

"Sister, are you well?" he asked in a soft voice. He glanced at the tent and then back to her. "It is the middle of the night and you should rest while you can."

At least he seemed to understand how inexperienced and uncomfortable she was on this journey. Not like the brute that led their group. He drove them on and on with a single-mindedness that shocked her. She was used to being in charge and the change in her circumstances was most likely the cause for her troubled state of mind. It was also the condition that kept thoughts tumbling around inside her mind and kept any hope of sleep at bay.

Sven cleared his throat, catching her attention, or rather her inattention, and she nodded her head.

"I need to walk a bit to work out some of the stiff-ness in my legs, if that is permitted?" she whispered back, trying to assume a meekness she did not feel. Men, she'd learned, liked women to act as though they had not a thought or plan in their heads.

Sven glanced across the camp and then back again. Their leader, Rurik, slept sitting up, wrapped in a dark cloak with his back against a tree. If Sven had not looked in that direction, Margriet certainly would never have spied him there.

Probably his intention.

When Sven held out his hand, she suspected Rurik had given some unseen signal granting his permis-sion. Margriet leaned on Sven's muscular arm as she let him guide her away from the tent. At first, they said nothing, but as they walked a short distance from the sleeping men, she could not contain her curiosity.

"Your leader does not seem happy about taking me back to Kirkvaw," she began.

Sven snorted and then answered. "Rurik is not happy about going back to Kirkvaw."

"What do you mean, sir? Will he not be rewarded for carrying out this task for my father?"

"Aye, he will be rewarded, but not by your father." Sven leaned in closer as though to share some con-fidence with her, but his disclosure was halted by a voice from the dark.

"Sven, you should not speak of such personal matters with Gunnar's daughter."

Margriet jumped at both the softness and the menace in his voice. Sven merely smiled and nodded at Rurik…and walked away as though silently ordered to do so.

Leaving Margriet in the company of the one person she would rather avoid.

He held out his arm and she placed her hand there. Without a word, he led her in a circle around their camp. Each step seemed easier than the last and finally the cramping in her back and hips ceased. Rurik did not stop guiding her until she drew to a halt when they passed her tent for the third time.

"My thanks, sir," she offered quietly as they stood next to the sleeping guard. She wondered why he did not rouse or reprimand the man for sleeping through her "escape." He must read thoughts, for he answered the question she did not speak aloud.

"He is there for your comfort, not your safety. If I thought there was true danger in this area, none would sleep."

"My comfort?"

"Aye. If you have need of anything, you should tell him." 'Twas then she noticed that the man did not sleep, but watched her and Rurik from his place on the ground. But the tone of his voice drew her gaze back up to Rurik's face.

The moon's light was bright that night, making it easy to see his expression, but that did not make it easy to understand it. Margriet would be willing to swear that he jested, but nothing she'd seen so far in his company spoke of a temperament familiar with anything less than complete seriousness.

"So, I should not step over him the next time I need to walk in the night?" The guard listened to their every word, but said nothing himself.

"Nay, Sister." He shook his head. "The next time you should wake him to say farewell." The guard now made a grunt that sounded much like a stifled laugh.

Perplexed by this change in his attitude and more curious than she'd like to admit, she decided to risk asking him the same question she'd ask Sven before he interrupted.

"So, 'tis true then? You do not wish to return to Kirkvaw?"

Actually, this was only her first question—she had many, many more about him and Kirkvaw and her father. This was only the beginning.

"I would ask you the same thing, Sister. Why do you not wish to return to Kirkvaw?"

She opened her mouth to argue, but the answer she would give and the one she should give were different and not something she wished to discuss with him. And her words would reveal, she worried, more than she wished anyone to know. Again, as though he read her thoughts, he replied before she could.

"Just so, Sister. Just so."

All Margriet could do was grit her teeth to keep from saying something, and she knew that whatever she said, 'twould not be good. Accepting defeat for the moment, she skirted around the guard, who had not moved, and crept back into the tent. When she adjusted the flap, she could see Rurik still standing outside, arms crossed over his chest, with his long cloak flowing over his broad shoulders and nearly reaching the ground.

In a low voice—one too soft for her to hear all the words exchanged—he spoke to the guard, who now did more than grunt. He spoke in the Norn of the common folk of the Orkneys and she struggled to understand. Although the lands around the convent had come under the rule of the Scottish lord Alexander de L'Ard a few years ago, Earl Erengisl was the primary sponsor of this and several other convents in Caithness. And people at his court spoke in the formal Norse of the royal court. Mother Ingrid, herself with origins from some other part of Scotland, had instructed her in the Gaelic tongue spoken here, but Margriet's talents lay in numbers and organization and not in skills with other tongues.

Rurik's words were calm and without anger and ended with a short, shared laugh, which she suspected was at her expense. When she leaned forward enough that he noticed her, Rurik, with an upward nod of his head, directed her back inside the tent. She blamed on her weariness that she did not argue or hesitate, but slipped back inside and lay down. This time her bones creaked but did not scream and she settled under the blankets as Elspeth slept on.

The sun rose earlier than it should have the next morning, or so it seemed to her, for she had only just closed her eyes when the order to break camp was shouted outside. At least she'd had the presence of mind to take the herbs she needed in the morning from her bag and place them within reach before she'd fallen asleep. Chewing them and drinking a sip of water as soon as she awakened helped calm her stomach from the ills that struck in the morn.

With no time for a lay-a-bed, Margriet prayed her stomach would settle and wished that it not repeat the occurrence of yestermorn as she folded the blankets. Taking slow, deep breaths as Cook had advised, she focused on her task and on her steps as she fought the waves of sickness welling and ebbing inside of her. If Elspeth noticed, she said nothing as they watched their tent being dismantled and packed. When handed a bowl of some kind of porridge by the man who guarded them through the night, her stomach rebelled.

Elspeth stayed close behind, thankfully waving off the men who followed, and warning in stronger a manner than she expected of the girl of the sisters' need to attend their personal needs. But when Margriet fell to her knees and emptied the meager contents of her stomach, she fell alone. The heaving continued even after its purpose was completed and it was several minutes before she sank back to sit on her heels and caught her breath.

Wiping her mouth, Margriet shuddered as the tremors calmed. The crackling of brush and leaves behind her alerted her to Elspeth's approach. Pushing up onto her feet, she turned to thank the girl for her assistance and instead found Rurik watching her from a few paces away. The hard lines of his face could have been carved from stone as he stared at her. His gaze moved over her and she could not move under his scrutiny.

"Sir?" Elspeth's voice shook, much as Margriet knew hers would if she attempted to speak at this moment.

She struggled against the strange hold she felt, one that made it difficult to breathe or to even look away from him. She reached up to make certain her wimple and veil were in place, for she feared she stood naked there in the light of day.

"Sir?" the girl asked again.

This time whatever spell had ensorcelled them dissipated and they both turned toward Elspeth…and Sven…and several of the others. Margriet took a deep breath and pulled her wits about her. Pushing past Rurik, she walked back toward the camp. When the others did not move to follow, she faced them and tried, with firm words, to distract them from the truth of the situation.

"Pray forgive my behavior, but I had great need of privacy."

Believing that the less said, the less chance of being tripped by an untruth, she turned back to the path through the trees. Silence still reigned behind her, but she continued hoping that it would be forgotten.

"And pardon us for intruding on that privacy, Sister."

Margriet nodded without turning, accepting his apology and trying to ignore the whispers that grew in loudness until she could make out a few of their words. 'Twas, however, Rurik's voice again that stopped her in her place.

"Your retching could be heard back in the camp, Sister. We feared for your well-being."

How should she handle this? His words gave her pause and the undercurrent of sarcasm confused her. Did she answer him now or should she wait until they could speak privately? Ignoring his challenge—and aye, it was one—could only cause more trouble. But what to say?

"My thanks, good sirs, for your concern and your assistance," she said as she met each of their gazes, with *his* being last. "I fear I have not traveled often nor do I travel well and 'twould seem that my body rebels against it."

He allowed her explanation to go without comment, for he was not yet certain what bothered him most about it—the need for it because of some condition of hers he knew not of, or that he thought it all a lie. Her hasty run from the camp, the sounds of retching that disturbed the quiet of the forest or the way her eyes took on a hazy look when she met his gaze. His gut liked none of those things, but the possibility that she lied intrigued him in a way he did not expect.

Rurik waved most of the men back to their duties, but he motioned to Sven and Magnus to remain. The lady's well-being must be a concern and her illness two days in a row did not bode well for their journey. They—he—could not arrive at Gunnar's house with his daughter in a cart, nearly dead from the trip. If she was to survive the journey and he to complete his task successfully, he must take her condition under consideration.

"Get your maps and meet me back in camp," he said. "I think our plans are too ambitious for Gunnar's daughter."

"At least your boots were not the target this morn," Magnus offered. "If Sister Margriet is this bad on land, how will she be during our sea voyage to the islands?"

Rurik looked one to the other and found the same grimace on both Sven and Magnus that he knew his own face wore. Still, he could recognize the problem here and forcing the woman at too quick a pace would simply lead to failure. In spite of his own delays at getting to this task, Rurik knew there was still plenty of good traveling weather before the winter's winds and storms made the sea over which they would travel nearly impassible. So, a slower journey, a few more days on the road to accommodate the most important one in their group, would not be of significance.

"Get your maps."

It took little time to review their planned path and decide how and where to break up their traveling. The convent was built at the southwestern edge of Caithness, in a place where the border shifted with each new lord. Initially, they were heading east to the coast, just south of where Caithness lands began, for the road, truly no more than a dirt path, would lead them past several small villages where they could replenish their provisions.

The northernmost Caithness lands, just before they reached the edge of the northern sea, was empty moorland, no forests to shelter beasts or plants that could feed them, so following the rivers or coast made more sense. It would take them several days more by that route, but it was still safer than traveling by sea along that section of the north coast. Fish and fowl would be available to them in and along the rivers they would follow, and more than make up for the additional days in their journey. At least, the land would be flat and not the arduous climbing needed to get out of these mountains that surrounded the convent.

After sending the men off to finish preparations for their day's journey, Rurik glanced over to see the two women sitting on a fallen tree. Although both wore the same clothing, the same garb marking them as part of a religious community, he still could not picture Margriet as living there. The flash in her eyes, when challenged or angry, was certainly not the patient acceptance he would expect in someone who had taken vows of obedience. And the way her hips swayed as she walked. Or the waves of raven hair that he knew still tumbled around her shoulders and down her back did not speak to him of someone who would live willingly under a vow of celibacy.

Turning to look at the men around him, Rurik realized that he seemed the only one affected by her in this manner. The others spoke to her in respectful voices, never meeting her gaze for more than a moment or two, never reaching out to touch her hand, and never staring at her the way he did. All treated both of them with the respect deserved and owed to women of the cloth.

Except him.

Regardless of his efforts to accept the situation as presented to him, he saw only a vibrant young woman who was wasted on the church. But, accept it he must, for his task was simply to return her to her father and be done with her. There were plans even now being made for his future and he doubted they would include the daughter of Gunnar, even though he was the High Counselor.

Aye, and if truth be told, plans were in place for the lady as well. Not royalty, her father was a rich and powerful man in his own right and he also served the Earl of the Orkneys and, in his name, ruled there when Erengisl was at his other properties or on some mission for the king.

From what he could glean from Sven's and Magnus's words and tales, Erengisl would be leaving the Orkneys for more important things, situations within the kingdom that needed his political insight and power, and he wished to leave one of his sons in Kirkvaw, and to place the other in charge of several of their properties in the Viipuri province and their family seat in Näsby.

Watching as Margriet reached out her hand in a graceful motion and accepted a cup of ale from one of the men, he realized that their fathers were the same—neither from royal blood but both had amassed wealth and power by serving those who were. And Rurik knew that they were much the same as well, for they would both be a pawn in their fathers' larger plan. For all his ruminations he almost missed her actions at just that moment. He stepped back nearer to the trees so that his presence would not alert her that he was watching her.

Very discreetly, she reached into a pocket in her tunic and then put whatever was there in her mouth. He could almost feel her holding her breath as she chewed on *something*. And when she thought no one was looking, she poured most of the ale in her cup into Sister Elspeth's. Then, she took a small cloth square and wrapped the chunk of bread and wedge of cheese given her to break her fast in it. She covered her furtive movement by hiding the bundle in her pocket with her motion rising from her seat.

Rurik thought it interesting. She did not eat the food he provided, but hid it away for…what? Later? For someone else? Sister Elspeth ate her food, slowly and steadily, but every morsel and drop given her was consumed. She asked not for more, so he would think her contented by it. Sven called to him across their encampment and he strode over to him, pushing the questions aside to handle the more pressing needs of his duties.

A short time later, he glanced over to see the women being helped onto their horses and he caught a glimpse of the joy on her face when she noticed the extra blankets folded as padding to soften the effects of riding long hours. Her gaze moved to his without a moment's delay and he found himself once more contemplating the womanly curves of the one beneath the garb.

And as the corners of her mouth tilted up in a gentle smile, his breath stopped in his chest. But when she licked her lips and mouthed the words *many thanks,* his body shuddered and hardened so quickly he thought he'd been struck by Thor's Hammer.

He realized in that moment that this journey was fraught with dangers he'd never considered when he agreed to the task. What kind of a man would lose control over a nun?

Rurik gave the signal for everyone to mount up and, within minutes, they were moving away from the clearing and back into the forest. He allowed Sven to take the lead, preferring to lag behind and consider his irrational actions.

Lusting after a nun? Was he daft?

Mayhap too many years of loving women, for he did love women, had brought him to this? He'd loved and touched and lusted after every sort of woman since he arrived in Scotland and began his life with his uncle's people. Once awakened, his appetite grew.

In spite of the fact that his ancestors' history of going *a-viking* and taking property and women—

whether willing or no'—had died long ago, he'd never bothered to correct those living under the protection of the MacLerie who still believed it. And since that reputation handed down through generations continued among them, Rurik had tried his best to live up to the expectations of those willing to be wooed.

'Twas said he rarely slept alone, but he never took a woman who did not wish to be taken and that was true. But, once her willingness was clear and consent given, there were no restraints between them.

Rurik took in a deep breath of cool, mountain air and let it out, watching the column of riders ahead of him moving down the worn path and remembering in that moment some of the best of times and the best of women in his past. A wave of sadness passed through him as Nara's image came to mind.

Regardless of his reputation and the wild stories told of his womanizing ways, when Rurik was with a woman who expected faithfulness, he was. He and Nara had been together for almost three years when his father's first call had come. Whether that was behind her leaving, he knew not. He'd shared with her alone the truth of his life with his father, and only kenned that, before his friends returned the second time, she left both him and Lairig Dubh behind to travel to her own family in a distant village.

As their time on the road passed and he allowed himself to wallow in these unfamiliar maudlin feelings, he noticed that Margriet now shifted on her mount and took something from her pocket. As she tried to adjust to the movements of the horse beneath her, the small bundle nearly went loose. Grabbing for it, she held it close and he could tell she ate it in small bites. If anyone glanced at her at that moment, they could not tell what she was doing. He knew.

He knew because nothing she did escaped his gaze.

Not a thing.

Not the way her mouth curved when she spoke.

Not the way her hand lightly touched the surface of everything she could as they passed by.

Not the way her voice grew husky as she whispered her prayers over meals or before sleeping.

Not a cursed or blessed thing.

Realizing what he did, Rurik closed his eyes and begged forgiveness from the Almighty. Not the many gods of his ancestors, but from the One who truly ruled the heavens and earth.

For he was a man whose heart missed the one woman he'd allowed himself to love even while his body lusted after a nun.

Chapter Five

Nary a hint of a breeze offering a respite from the encasing heat of the habit she'd chosen to wear passed over her. Margriet cursed her own foolishness as sweat gathered on her brow and trickled under the wimple to trace a path down her neck, between her shoulders and onto her back. This was one aspect of her disguise she'd not thought through.

She expected that the habit would offer protection from the untoward advances of the men in the traveling group, and it had. The men treated her and Elspeth with deference and respect and kept a decent distance from them. None seemed to even consider that they were not nuns. None but their leader, for she caught him watching her at the oddest moments and suspected he knew something was amiss.

Or mayhap 'twas her own guilty conscience over the matter?

Her plan made sense; even the reverend mother

seemed to agree that it was sound. That was before the journey began, before they left the enclosed valley that surrounded and protected the convent and its lands with an abundance of forests and streams… and blessed shade! They'd left the valley the morning before and still crossed a piece of land that offered nothing but flat, hard ground and nothing growing save for some short bushes and ground-hugging plants.

Aye, her plan *had* made sense at the beginning. However, the heat had not been one of her concerns and she did not ever remember any of the sisters complaining of it. Yet another bit of proof that she would never be suitable for the religious life. Then, as though he sensed her unspoken acknowledgement, Rurik turned and met her gaze. The moisture increased on her face and now she could feel it trickle down between her breasts. Made worse by her hair, now tucked under her tunic to hide its length, Margriet considered that mayhap she'd chosen the wrong course of action.

Again.

As always.

She sighed and turned her eyes from his. Reaching into her sleeve, Margriet tugged a square of linen free and dabbed at the sweat that threatened to soak her if left untended. It was very difficult to attain the same attitude of unruffled calm that the nuns seemed to have, especially when the clouds cleared above and the sun offered more heat than they needed this day. Looking around for Elspeth, she noticed the girl seemed to like it even less than she did herself. Touching the cloth to her forehead, Margriet wondered if the girl would keep her silence…and their secret until the journey's end.

"Sister?"

Margriet turned to discover that Sven rode now at her side. He was the most pleasant of the men and he was always considerate of her comfort. "Have you need of something to drink?" He held out a skin and offered its contents to her.

"Many thanks, Sven," she said as she accepted it, took several swallows and then held it out to him. The water was not cold, but it refreshed her nonetheless. He passed it over to Elspeth, who partook of it as well.

"You might wish to pour some on your cloth and cool your face," he said and then the man blushed as he realized he spoke of something probably more personal than a man should to a nun. He stammered a moment or two before he got the words out. "My pardon, Sister, but your face is very red and I thought you might be…uncomfortable."

Trying to lessen his embarrassment, Margriet replied, "I thank you for such concern for my well-being. I would not want to waste our supply on such a selfish thing, no matter that 'twould be a welcome relief in this heat."

Fearing that her words did not sound religious enough, she added, "And I offer such suffering up in the name of Our Lord." She raised her eyes heavenward and then closed them for a moment, mimicking the gesture she'd witnessed hundreds, nay, thousands of time during her years at the convent.

Margriet did unfold the cloth and try to find a dry patch to absorb the gathering beads of sweat. She knew not of the plans for their journey, but hesitated to use their water for her own comfort. Again, the thought that she'd made a mistake crossed her mind. Sven nodded and offered the water to them again, and after each took a few sips, he urged his horse into a quicker pace than she could maintain and took his place at the front of the group.

Where *he* rode this day.

She realized she was the topic of conversation when Rurik turned to look back at her and then shared more words with Sven. Margriet had barely a few minutes to wallow in her discomfort when Sven returned to her side.

"We will reach a river soon, so you should not worry over using the water to cool your brow," he said.

Caught by her own lying words, Margriet fretted over what to do. The part of her that was melting in the heat wanted to grab up the skin and pour every drop of the remaining water over her head. But, the part of her that usually thought things through triumphed in this and she allowed him to pour a few drops on the linen, before dabbing her brow and cheeks with it.

"Many thanks for your consideration, Sven. I admit that this heat is unexpected and a trial."

He moved his horse to walk next to hers and took

the water skin from her. The group still moved at the same pace, but 'twas a slower one than they'd maintained the first two days of their journey. Those days were lost in a fog, for she could only remember the misery of leaving the convent behind and the pain of traveling on the back of a horse.

Her journey to the convent all those years ago she did not remember at all, having only eight years and mourning the loss of her mother. So, having naught with which to compare, she thought this journey must surely be the worst of her life.

She waited for the man to speak and when he did not, she fell quiet, sinking back into her thoughts of the journey ahead and the repercussions of her fall from grace. Sven drifted back to a place next to Elspeth and she could hear his words as he stumbled over the correct pronunciation of the words in Elspeth's Gaelic tongue.

Looking at the rest of the men, she only then realized that they were a mix of Scots and those from her homeland in the Orkneys. Rurik, Sven, Magnus and six more sounded clearly at home with both the formal court language and that of the common people. Four of the others, as well as Elspeth, spoke only Gaelic.

Rurik was the only one who spoke all three.

Glancing ahead, she watched his silhouette as he guided the travelers along this road. Tall and muscular, both on and off his mount, he spoke little and gave few orders, yet there was no doubt that he commanded this group. Both the Scots and those from

Orkney attended to his words and directions with a quiet acceptance, as one does with an acknowledged leader, much as the sisters did with the reverend mother.

The other thing she noticed about him was that he remained apart, from nearly everyone including Sven and Magnus. Those two—she glanced over at Sven, who was still speaking, or rather trying to, with Elspeth—were friends of long-standing. She could tell by their easy manner with each other. They also seemed to have some connection to Rurik, for they spent time with their heads together, plotting and planning, each day.

But what about Rurik?

As though her thoughts had spoken his name, he turned back and met her gaze. Margriet touched the linen to her face once more and looked away, unable or unwilling to face his intense scrutiny. There would be time on this journey to discover his secrets. Sven knew something about him and his reasons for over-seeing her return and had referred to it while they walked in camp that first night. Before Rurik interrupted his words…

So, there were secrets here to be discovered!

As always happened when faced with a task, Margriet's mind began to swirl and plan the best way in which to accomplish it. By the time they reached the river's edge, she saw all the steps in the path to finding out who Rurik was and his reasons for taking on the mission of bringing her home.

* * *

The place chosen for their stop that night was pleasant. Looking around the area near her tent and the central fire, Margriet noticed the branches of the trees moving in the breezes that soothed her after the heat of the day. Any relief was certainly dulled by the layers of clothing she wore, but 'twas still more comfortable than the midday sun's glaring rays when there was no shade to blunt them.

Now, sitting on a stool fashioned from the stumps of some fallen trees and eating a surprisingly well-cooked stew, Margriet watched as the men broke off into smaller groups divided, as near as she could tell, by language and origin. The Scots sat away from the fire, passing a skin of ale between them, while those from the north sat nearer.

Rurik did not eat, but paced around the camp, checking horses and supplies. Seeing an opportunity, she rose and went to the fire. Dipping the long-handled spoon in the cooking pot, she scooped out a serving of the food and carried it to where he stood now. His surprise sat plainly on his face, but he nodded and took it from her.

"You need not serve me, Sister," he said before accepting an eating spoon that she also carried to him.

"I have so little to do, sir. Other than pray, of course. And 'tis the least I can do to show my appreciation."

He ate a few more mouthfuls without saying another word. Sven walked over with a battered cup and a skin of ale, which he held out to Rurik. Handing her his bowl and spoon, she watched as he first poured some into the cup before offering it to her, while he simply opened his mouth and filled it with ale from the skin. After passing it back to Sven, Rurik took back his food and ate it in silence.

Margriet sipped from the cup as she considered which questions to ask first. If she were too aggressive, he would back away. Too soft in her approach and he would wile his way out of answers that would enlighten her about him and his past.

"Why do you not wish to escort me to my father?"

"Pardon?" he asked, stopping with his spoon halfway between the plate and his mouth.

"'Tis clear to me that you do not want this duty. Why did you agree to it then?" She lifted the cup to her lips and forced another sip, trying with all her might to remain calm and pursue her intentions to discover more about him.

She'd caught him by surprise, she could tell. His eyes widened even as his mouth stopped chewing the food in it. He tried to swallow then, but Margriet knew he would choke.

And he did.

When his breath collided with that food, he convulsed with loud coughs. The plate flew through the air as he leaned over and, with his hands on his thighs, tried to loosen the blockage from his throat. Without stopping to think, Margriet ran to his side and began pummeling him on his back.

A few minutes went by before he stopped choking

and she continued delivering blows until he did. After what seemed to be ages of time had passed, he waved her off and Margriet stepped back. 'Twas then she noticed the quiet that surrounded them.

To a person, everyone in the camp stood, mouths agape, staring at them. No one moved as she adjusted her wimple back to where it should sit on her head and as she tugged her robes back in place. When she had regained her composure and her breath, for beating the warrior's back with her bare hands was hard work, she cleared her own throat and turned back to Rurik.

"Are you well now?" she asked.

"Now that I can breathe again or now that you have stopped trying to pound me into the ground?" Sarcasm laced his words and the sting of it slashed at her.

Humiliation pulsed through her body, making her heart pound in her chest and bringing the heat of embarrassment to her face. Worse, she felt the burning of tears in her eyes and her throat, forcing her to look away from him.

Why had she thought that she could face down a man, and one such as this one, and get her way? Margriet lowered her head and turned, hoping to walk quickly to some darkened corner of the camp where she could wait until the horror of her actions dissipated or at least until everyone ceased staring. She'd only taken a few steps when his voice stopped her.

"Sister, my thanks for your assistance," he said loud enough for all to hear. Rurik watched as she stopped, unsure if she would still bolt, as the look in her eyes declared, or if she would remain. He waited and then held out his hand to her. "And my thanks for bringing me food."

He stepped closer, though not too close, and glared over her head at those who still gawped at her, ordering their gazes away with a nod of his head. Only the little nun still watched, though hers was a look of concerned observation rather than a curious one.

Rurik had not realized his words were as harsh as they were until he saw the horror and embarrassment fill her face. 'Twas the tears he spied in the last moment before she fled that undid him. When she still did not take his hand, he bent over and picked up the cup she'd been drinking from and motioned to Sven for the skin of ale. Once filled, he offered it to her.

Margriet took a sip and then another, and he waited in silence while she regained her wits. Well, if the truth were told, she'd not lost her wits, only her control. He suspected that losing control was something that did not happen often to the lady, nun or no'. Instead of staring at her now pale face, he turned back to the task he'd left when she'd brought him food— checking the supplies for the next day's journey.

After seeing her distress on the first days of their travel, he'd agreed to several changes in their plans. First, they broke the distance into small bits so that they could travel more slowly each day. Second, they changed their route, deciding to follow more of the rivers north then across the coast to the village of Thurso, where they would take a boat to Orkney. Third, although they carried most of their food with them, they now sent men ahead to the small settlements along their path to barter for fresh food and necessities.

Although his assignment was to bring her home, he had only the wild seas and winds of winter to limit his time to do that. That might be stretching it a bit thin, but he knew any arrangements would wait until their return and so the only rushing he did was that which he wished to do.

Or so he told himself over and over again since meeting the woman called Gunnar's daughter.

She moved behind him and he turned to face her. In that moment, watching her eyes and her expression as they changed from dark and untrusting to something more open and welcoming, he knew he must answer her question.

"Returning you to your father is my duty, one I accepted and will carry out as requested. Duty though is no' always conveniently timed and that is my hesitation."

Could she hear the lie in his words? This was a duty he did not want and—even more now that he'd met her—one that he regretted. She had not wanted to leave the convent, as she said over and over again, but she had no choice in the matter. Her father called her home to her duties to their family and honor.

As his called him.

His explanation pleased her at some level, for she raised her face to him now, not cowering or hiding any longer. The light of the setting sun behind him brightened her eyes and made her lips look fuller and softer. She spoke again, now, and this time her voice strengthened to what he knew it could be.

"You speak the Highland tongue as though you were born to it," Margriet said. "Are you Scot and not from Norway or Sweden?"

"My mother is Scottish, from the west."

Rurik decided that was all he need reveal. In spite of the offer relayed to him by Sven and Magnus, he would believe it only when the words came from his father's mouth. Allegiances changed. Arrangements changed. No need to hold himself up to shame if more promises were broken.

She did not ask another question, but seemed to think on his words. Sipping from the cup, she watched him as he continued his inspection. When he stepped away, she followed, never missing a thing he did. Finally, when the constant observation irritated him, he looked at her.

"Is there something you need, Sister?" he finally asked. "I cannot pay attention to the task at hand if I am conversing with you."

"Nay," she said with a shake of her head.

The wimple that had tilted precariously while she beat his back was now back in place, hiding the hair he knew would be bouncing around her shoulders if freed from its constraints.

Great Frey's Eyes, he lusted after a nun! With each attempt to rein it back and tamp it down, it reared again with the slightest gesture that reminded him of the woman beneath the garb. A shake of her head and he was lost? How could he have so little control?

When he thought she would return to her meal and the others, she did not. Instead, she finished the ale in one tilt of the cup and then looked at him.

"I wished to walk to the river and need your permission," she said. The lowering of her head for a moment would have appeared to anyone watching as acquiescence, however only he could see the flash of anger that darkened her eyes to a darker shade of blue.

Margriet Gunnarsdottir did not ask anyone's permission to do anything, they seemed to say, and he suspected it for the truth. Rurik nearly laughed at her attempt to placate him, but decided this bore watching.

"Sven, come!" he yelled. When his friend approached, he pointed at Margriet. "Escort the sisters to the river's edge. There might be a cooling breeze there to ease the heat."

She spoke no words of thanks to him. She said nothing at all and only granted him the smallest of nods in exchange for the consent she sought. Rurik knew the area was safe, for both he and his men had searched it thoroughly before setting up their camp. And, if she were gone, he could finish his work before the sun set.

Or so he told himself.

And that was but another lie heaped on the ones he already said or thought. He'd been living a lie for years, portraying the man those with whom he lived and fought next to expected him to be, and he'd lost the man he truly was. His sudden arrival without explanation at his uncle's holding, his upbringing in Sweden and Norway and on the Orkneys and his appearance—tall, blond, strong—all helped him create the facade of a Viking warrior of legend. He resisted a smile as he remembered but a few of the women and their reactions to him. On the verge of full manhood, their brazen interest in his growing sexual prowess spurred him on and he discovered that he loved women…and they loved him.

Now, he must find the truth of the real man within before confronting his father and the demands that family and honor required. Still though, his practiced behavior of the last ten years was more comfortable than examining his character, and so he found himself watching the sway of her hips as she walked away.

His gaze followed them—her—as Sven led the women across the camp and toward the river. Sister Elspeth walked with her head down, in prayerful contemplation or in her usual silence he knew not, and in a demeanor closer to what he thought a nun's should be. The young woman only spoke to Sven, who seemed intent on learning her Gaelic. Rurik shook his head and turned back to his task.

Why Sven bothered himself with the effort he could not understand, for there could be nothing between them and Rurik knew that Sven would not return to this or any part of Scotland. But the young sister laughed softly and corrected Sven's mangling of the words he tried to say. He decided there was no harm in it. After all, learning another tongue was no' such a bad way to spend the time on the journey.

A few minutes passed and Rurik mastered his lack of control and completed his inspection. Night approached, but the morn would find them ready to travel. He wanted to take advantage of the fair weather they had now before reaching the blustery and stormy northern edge of the country.

As they traveled farther, the conditions would surely deteriorate and their progress would be slowed. No more summery days with heat like this. No' many days of full sun beating down from above. Nay, he expected that the rain showers and winds of the far north would greet them soon. He surveyed the gathering once more and was about to see if any stew remained in the pot when her scream pierced the calm.

Rurik pulled the sword ever at his side from its scabbard on his belt and took off in a full run, calling out instructions to the men as he passed them. Branches slapped at his face and arms as he pushed through the dense brush. He ran not on the path where the women had walked, but into another area so that his arrival at the river would not be where expected. Better to surprise an attacker than give them the advantage of knowing where you would be.

The scene that met him as he reached the river's edge was like something from one of the farcical entertainments that Jocelyn planned at Lairig Dubh.

One nun sprawled out in the water, the other standing on the edge trying to reach her. Sven standing nearby, laughing like a madman, not helping at all. Then, before he could do anything, the second nun went flying into the water as well. His men crashed through the bushes and circled the bank of the river waiting for his orders.

Sven caught sight of them first and frowned at him. Then the two women, both now mostly under water save for their wimpled heads that bobbled on the surface, noticed them standing at the ready for battle. Rurik could tell the exact moment when Margriet realized that she was the cause of their presence. And their fully armed presence at that. The obvious enjoyment left her face in a rush and she tried to stand up.

"What is amiss here?" he called out.

"Sister Margriet slipped and fell into the water. Sister Elspeth reached out to help her, and you see what happened," Sven offered, all the while not looking the least bit concerned for either of them. Rurik sent the rest of the men back to the camp and walked closer. "The river flows softly in this spot and they are in no danger."

Still, it was unseemly for two nuns to be paddling around in the pool formed where the river made a turn. And instead of expressing outrage or fear at the occurrence, they remained in the water for several minutes before swimming over the shallow edge and beginning to climb out. After slipping back into the water twice, each time with a splash and a now-tempered laugh, they managed to climb out.

The whole incident was quite…unsisterly. He'd never known nuns who would take part in such folly and play. He'd never known nuns that reveled in falling in a river and did not scream for help. He'd never known nuns like this…well, actually, now that he thought on it, he'd never known nuns.

Shaking his head, he could not decide if he should help or not. However, when the increased weight of the soggy layers of clothing made it difficult for the women to walk, Rurik sheathed his sword—the one he now noticed he yet brandished in his hand—and strode over to assist them. They should remove their sodden clothes before the chill of the night set in and they took ill from this mishap.

As he reached out for Margriet's hand, he caught sight of her shoes and stockings placed carefully away from the water's edge. He caught her eye and saw in the amused glimmer there that this was no accident. She veiled her expression quickly and looked away, but too late. Rurik knew in his gut that she had fallen into the river on purpose. And the other sister as well.

He would ask Sven about this once the women were settled in their tent for the night. And he would keep watch over their behavior on the rest of the trip for something surely was awry. Sven's words as he passed only confirmed it.

"Puir wee women of God," he said in Gaelic with an accompanying tsk.

Apparently Sven was learning a new tongue, but not a thing about women.

Puir wee women indeed.

Chapter Six

The foolishness of the risk seemed worthwhile when the cool water soaked through the layers of heavy cloth and hit her overheated skin. But the true pleasure came when she dunked her head, wimple and veil and all, under the cold surface. If no one had been watching, she would have ripped the constraining layers off and let her skin feel the rush of the soothing wetness directly.

Truly, the first thought she had was to only remove her shoes so that they would not be ruined, but the sight of the cool water flowing by made her lose all thoughts of being circumspect. The day had been one constant stream of sweat—beading and trickling, beading and pouring—under the rough clothes she wore, and her finer chemise could not protect her from the coarseness against her skin.

But the cold water had soothed her. Now, as Rurik assisted her back to the camp, she wondered if this had been a grievous error on her part. He'd said not a word as she stopped to retrieve her shoes from the side of the path where she'd left them, but his expression darkened and she was tempted to move away from his side. They reached the small tent and he waited for them to enter.

"Hand out your wet garments and I will spread them over some bushes to dry. It feels like a mild night. They should be dry by morning."

The words were rote, but they carried such an ominous undertone that Margriet worried she'd crossed over some line. And mayhap she had?

"My thanks, sir," she said, allowing Elspeth to enter first. Meeting first the gaze of one and then the other, she continued, "I did not mean to cause such a problem for you over such a small thing."

Hoping that her words would salve his conscience, she bent down to enter the tent.

"You jumped in," he whispered so that only she would hear.

"I fell in, sir."

"You pulled Sister Elspeth in."

"She lost her balance trying to help me, sir," she placated. Apparently he'd seen more than she thought. The water trickling down from her sodden hair was not soothing any longer.

"As you say, La…Sister," he growled.

Margriet turned and quickly pulled the flap down between them. Elspeth had already taken off the gown and tunic and veil and wimple, and held them out to her. She in turn held them through the flap until he took them.

"Pray, one moment, sir, and I will hand out mine."

No sound came in reply, but Margriet hastened to untie and remove her garments. With Elspeth's help, she finished quickly and held them out through the flap of the canvas to him. They were taken from her grasp without another word, but Margriet would have taken an oath that she'd heard coarse words being muttered as they were.

Once that task was done, to her surprise, two drying cloths were tossed in to them. She sat down and pulled her small bag out, searching for her comb until she found it. With a motion to keep quiet, Margriet handed the comb to Elspeth and they spent a short while combing and braiding each other's hair. She discovered that sitting in her damp chemise was much more comfortable than the nun's habit and soon, the traveling and the weariness she now felt each day grew until she gave in and lay down on the blankets arranged on the ground.

After she readied the items she needed first in the morning, Elspeth handed their small lantern out to the now present guard. The sun's light quickly disappeared and the quiet of night crept in and surrounded them. Her body was exhausted, but the questions and problems began tormenting her and her mind could not let go of them.

Did Rurik know she was not a nun? He was not a stupid man and she knew her efforts at keeping up her disguise were not the best. Margriet examined her reasons for even trying and found that she still needed to continue the subterfuge. Or did she?

Observing his treatment of her and Elspeth, she was beginning to doubt that they were in danger of lechery by him or his men on this journey. Granted, the men believed them to be nuns and that belief probably held back the worst of their words and actions. Rurik seemed to command the men and none seemed interested in breaking his rules.

She could not, absolutely could not, return to her father's house in this garb unless she planned on entering the convent and taking her vows. Her father would not understand and she needed to find Finn so they could speak to her father to gain his permission to marry. If her father announced any plans for her future, she would be bound by his decision and her condition would bring shame to his honor.

So, at some point in the journey she must reveal herself to Rurik and make him understand her predicament. Would Rurik help her? He spoke only of a duty to be performed. Could he understand the plight of a man and woman in love? She thought not.

The next problem, not borrowing trouble but simply trying to sort things out in her mind, was about her condition. The herbs did help a bit in the morning and made her sickness just bearable as long as she had time to chew them before rising. Now though, her breasts ached and seemed swollen and the shape of her belly was changing. The old cook had warned her to expect such things and more in the coming weeks as her body adapted to the bairn growing inside.

Caught. That was what she'd heard whispered about girls who shared themselves with men before betrothal or marriage and got with child. And so she was and would be called if the truth became known. Margriet could only hope that Finn would be true to his word and was already putting things in order so that he could make the arrangements for their marriage with her father.

And he did love her. She knew it in her heart and believed his pledge to her to be as strong as any betrothal. Finn loved her and when she promised herself, body, heart and soul, to him that night, she did so because she believed his words. He was a wealthy merchant and would be acceptable to her father as a husband for her. He would marry her and they would raise the bairn together. He did love her and would stand by her.

Margriet's heart began to pound and her stomach churned as the bitter taste of doubt entered her thoughts. Then why had he disappeared so swiftly? Why had he left without a word and without giving her some token of his love and vows? Something had changed between them when a messenger arrived from the south and, within two days, he was gone.

She wished she had some confidante with whom she could share her worries and fears and her hopes. Certainly the nuns at the convent were not about to listen to her stories of love and virtue surrendered. Even when she spoke to the cook, a woman who had borne five children, she could not bring herself to mention matters of the heart, for she was of a noble family and her father's status was one of honor and high standing and...

And she should have known better than to lie with a man outside the bounds of holy matrimony.

Apparently, the extensive education she'd received in the language arts, mathematics and even some topics thought unnecessary for a woman did not prepare her for the emotional onslaught of a charming, handsome, rich young man intent on pursuing passion. So long ignored by family so far from home, she'd lost the ability for all logical reasoning when faced with his pledges of love and promises of a future together.

Finn answered all her questions about the world outside the walls of the convent and made her feel important and loved for the first time since before her mother died and she'd been exiled here. And if she'd been a little infatuated or had not seen the folly in her actions, well, she could understand it now as she looked back on those magical days.

Margriet rolled to her side and tucked her hand under her cheek. Remembering the thrill of passion in his touch and in his kisses, she felt her lips tingle and her core pulse with life and heat. How could she have resisted when he did things she'd never known could happen between a man and woman? Even now, when doubts raced through her, her body responded to just the memories of it.

Men were truly strange creatures—honorable when it suited their purposes, strong when they must be and subtle when guile worked over force. They did not think as a woman thought or expect the same things in life as a woman wanted and needed. Watching the men who escorted her now, Margriet could see more of the differences between men and women and also among the group of men. With her only exposure to the opposite gender being those men who lived on the convent grounds—old ones, blind ones, crippled ones—seeing these young, healthy, hardy, muscular warriors afeared of nothing and no one gave her pause.

So, could she not be forgiven for not having that understanding and wisdom when she'd met Finn to realize the kind of man he was? Surely the Almighty would consider it even if her father did not?

The pitiful ache in her stomach grew as she felt the doubt grow inside. Each thought and memory brought with it recognition and revelation…and guilt and shame. Reaching in her bag, she took some of the herbs and tucked them inside her cheek, waiting for them to soften so she could chew on them. She brushed away the tears that flowed and tried to quiet the upset within her.

Margriet was not accustomed to self-pity and she blamed this bout of it on her exhaustion and her fears. Torn from the only place she remembered as her home and taken back to people and places she could not recall, 'twas no wonder she was falling victim to such doubts and terrors.

Just when she calmed herself down with some deep breaths, shouting broke the silence of the night. She sat up and began to reach for the flap when the guard spoke. He must have heard her rustling around in the tent.

"Just some of the men in the river, sisters. Naught to worry about." Leathen, one of the Scottish men in the group, chuckled then. "Apparently your mishap gave them an idea."

"My thanks for watching over us, Leathen," she said. Then, for good measure, she added in a solemn tone, "May God bless you."

Hopefully, the man did not hear Elspeth's giggle, muffled by the blanket she held over her mouth as she did so. So, the girl did not yet sleep, either. As though hearing her thoughts, Elspeth whispered softly, "All will be well, Lady Margriet."

It was the girl's gentle patting of Margriet's hand that gave her comfort, and finally she lay back down and fell to sleep.

'Twas when the lantern light threw her shadow on the side of the tent that Rurik knew he was losing the battle once more.

His body gave him all kinds of messages and warnings as he watched the silhouette undress before him. He did not need to see inside—his mind filled with images of his own making. Having helped her onto and down from her horse, watched her walk and then seen the garments plastered to her skin by the weight of the water, he did not need to see the reality in order to imagine how the feminine curves of her body would appear.

Ripe breasts that would fill his hands.

Hips wide enough to bear children.

Muscular but soft thighs to open in welcome to him.

He cursed then, in a low grumbling voice, letting out some of his frustration, not at what he saw but at what he allowed himself to imagine. Stepping back from the tent, he motioned to Sven and Magnus to follow. Then he walked back toward the river, flinging the soaking wet garments over various bushes as he passed them. If they landed in the dirt, he knew not, for he did not dare to pause when his desire was so strong.

Rurik reached the riverbank and stopped only long enough to remove his weapons and boots, breeches and tunic, before diving into the deepest area of the river. Luckily, the cold water did exactly what he needed it to do, so that when Sven and Magnus joined him, there was no evidence of his unholy urges.

They dove and surfaced, letting the cold water cool them for several minutes before Rurik finally swam to one of the rocks that was submerged at the river's edge. Sitting on it, he reclined mostly under the water. After the others followed, he spoke.

"Why did you allow her in the river?" he asked, rubbing his face. "Did she tell you of her plan?"

"Her plan?" Magnus asked, looking from one to the other.

"Aye, her fall was no accident," Sven admitted. "They asked if they could step in the water to cool their feet. What could I have done?"

"Said nay?" Rurik offered.

"There was no sign of danger and it seemed like such a little thing, so I said aye." Sven laughed. "I knew they were plotting something when they put their heads together as they removed their shoes. So, when Sister Margriet fell, I knew the other would also."

Sven swam away from the rocks now and dove back under the water. This water was cold, but they were all used to much colder, for they'd all swum in the sea at home. Rurik considered that Margriet's plan was a good one to relieve the heat of the day. At least he was not covered from foot to head in swaddlinglike garments and could simply remove his cloak when too hot. Not like the women—the nuns—who must, for decency's sake, remain covered. When Sven returned to the river's edge, Rurik thought it best to warn him.

"Do not be cajoled or misled from any order I give, Sven. Not even when the young one teaches you a new word or smiles at you."

Sven batted Magnus's arm and then met Rurik's gaze. "And I could warn you of the same thing with the other. You devour her with your every look."

He lunged without thinking, grabbing Sven by the throat and taking him down under the water. Sven did not make it easy, not with his words or actions, for the struggle went on until neither could hold their breath any longer. Gasping as they rose from the water, Rurik released him and flung himself aside to gain some distance and to gain some time to gather his control.

That Sven was right simply made it worse. That Rurik himself recognized his own weakness did not help. Now, with the words spoken, his lust for the nun would have to be acknowledged, at least among these friends.

"You saw her comely figure when she ran out without her habit on at the convent. That hair," he said, meeting Sven's gaze. "That face and body," he said, winking at Magnus. "But for her assurances that she has taken the veil, there is nothing about the woman that would declare her a nun."

And he realized that the problem had begun then, in that very moment when he'd seen her as a woman. Her defiance and challenge to him as he carried out his duty and then her respectful capitulation added to the appeal. No matter though, he had never taken a woman against her will or dallied with those who were virgins or married and he would not begin to now. In spite of his body's urges to the contrary. After the others joined him in his moment of appreciation, he knew it was time to put this aside, both within himself and among them.

"Old habits die slowly and not without a fight," he said to both of them. "Since I have been old enough to have hairs on my…chin, I have loved women. Nun or no', Margriet Gunnarsdottir is a woman and some things—" he paused and threw a glance down to the part of him in the water "—have not a care about her vows. But, those vows and my duties to her father and mine are a line I will not cross."

Magnus and Sven nodded in understanding and agreement, for lust was one thing, but violating one's honor was a completely other matter.

Rurik climbed from the water and picked up his clothes, making his way back to the camp without another word. He'd explained all he needed to explain and more than he wanted to, but admitting his reactions seemed to lessen them. Taking a deep breath of the cooling night air, Rurik felt in control and ready to face the challenges of the rest of the journey north.

Then he spied the sisters' habits strewn over the bushes where he'd thrown them and was stopped in his tracks.

She was sleeping without garments on this night. The cold water had brought a rosy glow to her skin, one he noticed on her face when he helped her from the water. Such a glow would cover not only her face but extend down onto her neck and her breasts and even her…

Sweet Freya's Tits!

As he pushed his way back through the trees to the camp, he fought the powerful urge that filled him and nearly made him change direction toward where she slept. In spite of his best efforts, he knew that the only thing that kept his feet on the path to the place where he'd left his supplies was the sound of Sven and Magnus following not far behind.

This night, when she had affected him so strongly, he would accept their presence and their knowledge of his weakness as the way to fight this attraction. Surely, in the light of day, he would have more strength.

Rurik tugged his breeches and tunic back on his damp skin and wrapped a blanket over his shoulders. Finding a tree with a broad trunk, he sat next to it, laid out his sword and two daggers within reach and then leaned back to rest. With a nod, he acknowledged the first two men serving as guards this night. They positioned themselves away from the remnants of the fire so they could see the whole camp. When Sven and Magnus gained their makeshift pallets, quiet descended and soon the air was filled with the sounds of night.

Fair fortune was with them, for the weather held for several more days, allowing the party to cover miles and make their way steadily north. The winds were cooler and there was no repeat of the incident that sent the nuns tripping, or jumping, in the river. Whether that was a good thing or no', Rurik debated, for he did not see that lighthearted side of Margriet over the next few days. The sickness plagued her each day, though she seemed to rally as they moved on.

Fight it though he did, he could not resist the urge

to watch her as they traveled. He was simply more circumspect about it so that others did not notice. Or he tried to be.

In many ways, she reminded him of Connor's wife, Jocelyn.

Capable.

Smart.

Kind.

And they both possessed an earthy kind of sensuality that drew men, although neither would admit to it or to their beauty.

Jocelyn swore she was plain of face, but if she ever saw the way her face glowed when she looked at Connor, she would realize how wrong she was. Margriet's habit hid most of her beauty, but having glimpsed it briefly, Rurik remembered the raven hair, framing the heart-shaped face with its flawless skin, entrancing eyes and lips meant to…

Ah, he did but repeat his error again, focusing on the facets of Margriet that drew him like a bee to nectar. He turned back to see how the women fared and allowed only a momentary inspection before the solution struck him.

When he met Jocelyn for the first time, he was infatuated with her. Of course, he'd not known that she was the laird's new wife when he'd snuck up behind her at the river's edge and attempted something more. But once the boundaries of their relationship were set, he and Jocelyn became friends, a good thing considering what happened to her those next weeks in Lairig Dubh as she and Connor struggled their way to happiness.

So, if befriending Jocelyn had helped him rid himself of the lustful feelings he had for her, mayhap it would work with Margriet? There were so many more reasons for trying it now, her vows, her father… his father. Possibly this would be a way around his body's reactions?

Rurik looked up at the sky, gauging the height of the sun and their journey so far this day. Leathen already rode ahead looking for an appropriate place to stop for the night. Tonight he would put his plan in action.

Chapter Seven

❦

The Earl's Hall
Kirkvaw

Thorfinn strode from the latest audience with his father and sought out his own chambers. The anger built inside until he was ready to destroy something… or someone. Slamming the doors behind him, he ordered the servants out and then did as he felt—the nearest table his target.

But, even knocking it over and spilling everything on it all over the floor did not relieve his frustration, so the lantern was next and then the pitcher of ale and the cups with it. Bashing them against the wall, spilling ale from one end of the chamber to the other simply increased his rage. He screamed out his anger.

The servant who entered the rooms then must have realized his mistake for he tried to leave. Thorfinn stepped in front of him and grabbed him by the tunic. Throwing him to the floor, he kicked him and ordered him to clean the mess. The damn fool deserved far more punishment, for he should know not to look at him in disrespect.

He, Thorfinn, was the legitimate son of Erengisl Sunesson and he should be inheriting everything. He should stand in his father's stead. He should be second to his father, representing him here or wherever needed. Instead, the bastard son had been called back to steal part of his inheritance and to steal the standing he should have as the *only* son, the only son that mattered.

Thorfinn tugged his cloak from his shoulders and tossed it on the floor. When the impudent servant stared at him once more, it took only a few swiftly delivered blows before the man learned his place— on the floor, at Thorfinn's feet. Only the knock at the door spared him further attention. Pushing the servant aside, Thorfinn walked to the door and opened it himself. His man asked leave to enter.

"You are long overdue," Finn said, taking a deep breath. The rage was spent now—using his fists always relieved it—and he wanted to hear the news in private. "Get rid of him and get me wine."

As Sigurd summoned servants to fulfill his wishes, Thorfinn went over to the window and watched the ships in the busy harbor. His chambers overlooked the water and he could see merchant vessels and smaller sailing skiffs dot the surface of the waters. When the noises behind him subsided, he turned and held out his hand for the cup he'd ordered. Sigurd did not disappoint him in that, and Thorfinn hoped he would not in the task given him, either. For his own sake as well as Thorfinn's plans.

The table was righted and the papers and books replaced on its surface. The disciplined servant was gone as well, but the blood on the floor and the ale on the wall would need to be scrubbed later. Thorfinn sat in a chair and waited on Sigurd's report. A little punishment to one and all of his underlings behaved better, or so it seemed to him when Sigurd launched into a succinct and thorough account.

The bastard Rurik was on his way to Kirkvaw after several delays in receiving his father's call. Thorfinn smiled at the thought of those delays and how angry his father was over them. The bastard did indeed escort Gunnar's daughter back now and the slut was forlorn over "Finn's" sudden departure.

The best part, the part that made his heart pound in anticipation of the success of his plans, was that there were many signs that his debauching of her was successful. Sigurd's man had spoken directly to a woman at the convent who had, with a bit of strong-armed convincing, revealed the slut's condition.

Nothing would neutralize Gunnar more than the dishonor of his daughter. So many arrangements would be undone over it, so much respect lost by it, that Thorfinn knew it had been the right thing to do. And, although Gunnar would know he was behind it all, there was nothing the Erengisl's first counselor could do to expose him or his hand in it all.

And Gunnar deserved all the humiliation he got, for it was his persuasion that convinced his father to call the bastard home. It was Gunnar who suggested that Rurik was a good man to leave in charge and who could rule in his father's name. It was Gunnar who stole his birthright and his father's esteem from him and Gunnar would be made to pay.

Thorfinn clenched the cup so tightly in his hand that it left an imprint on his palm. He tried to calm the shaking as he drank deeply of the wine. His thoughts were filled with images of the lovely, but stupid Margriet.

Gunnar's daughter had walked right into "Finn's" arms, accepting his advances and talk of love and a future. Stupid slut that she was, she would be the instrument of her father's downfall. Even better and more satisfying, he would bring the bastard down as well and have done with all of them.

Now, all he had to do was wait for their arrival, planting seeds of distrust before they arrived and preparing for his own acceptance of his father's recognition.

Thorfinn drank the last of the wine and waved Sigurd off with orders to continue as they'd planned. When his gaze settled on the stained floor and wall, he realized these were just portents of things to come.

Blood would be spilled and bigger messes than this one would need to be put aright before he was done with Gunnar, his slut of a daughter and the bastard he'd chosen to support.

They deserved anything they got for being in his way.

Chapter Eight

Margriet watched as he circled the camp again. Everyone else sat near the fire and ate their food while he walked around them eating his. Somehow he'd managed to find another hot meal for them and, between the hearty fish stew and the coarse bread, it was flavorful and satisfying…and completely unexpected. When he'd come with his summons, she'd thought of being forced to eat dried berries and oats along the journey. So, each day's hot meal was a boon.

After almost six days traveling, they were only halfway to the coast, but her body was becoming more accustomed to riding now. Aye, she certainly ached by the end of the day and, truth be told, she did not think her bottom and legs would ever recover, however, each day was a bit easier than the last. Even the morning distress that plagued her on waking was subsiding and that was a very good thing.

Rurik passed her again, this time slowing as though

he planned to stop. At the last moment, he continued on, throwing a glance in her direction as he walked and mumbled something under his breath. Then, he abruptly turned and sat down next to her. His breadth and width took up much more of the improvised bench than she did, so Margriet gathered the folds of her habit closer to give him room on the fallen tree where she and Elspeth sat.

"I would speak to you about something," he began. "Sister," he added after that momentary hesitation that occurred every time he addressed her.

There was another longer pause before he spoke again. Margriet cleared her throat to encourage him to say what he came to say. Elspeth, she noticed, scooted as far as she could away from them to avoid being included. Margriet only wished she could do the same.

"I would beg a favor from you."

His expression was one of sheepish dismay, probably due to whatever the need was that forced him to ask her this. Rurik's face flushed red as he seemed to search for the words he needed. 'Twas then that she realized the others, not only Elspeth, but the other men also, had scrambled away from them, giving them a small measure of privacy.

Surely not a good sign.

"Sister, several of the men with us do not speak Norn, something they must do if they wish to stay in the Orkneys after our journey." He did not meet her gaze yet.

"And is that their intention?"

"Aye. Can you teach them?" he blurted out. "While we ride or when we stop for the night?" he added. His eyes reminded her of the cook's son when he'd done something wrong, the glimmer made him appear much younger than his…and made her curious.

"How many years have you?" she asked without stopping herself.

He shrugged and frowned, and Margriet thought he would not give her an answer. Then he looked at her and answered, "Twenty and six years."

"That is not so old then," she replied, then realized that it was impertinent to ask such a thing.

"And you, Sister? How many years have you?"

Startled that he would be so direct back to her, she answered. "Eight and ten years."

"Not so old, either."

"But you expected younger, did you not?" she asked as she remembered his words and his call to bring out the "girl."

He laughed then and his face brightened and softened in the most appealing manner. "You are correct, Sister. I had thought Gunnar's daughter to yet be a child. That detail was not given to me when the task to escort you was." He brushed his hands together, removing dust from them, and then he turned to look at her once more. "His letter spoke of his young daughter and instead I found a woman full grown."

Margriet felt the heat rise in her cheeks and she lowered her face. He said nothing more just then, but she could feel the heat of his gaze. A few moments passed and then he cleared his throat and gained her attention.

"You have not answered my question yet, Sister. Can you teach them Norn?"

"I…do not know," she offered. "I…" She hesitated to admit her lack of experience about the common language in the Orkneys.

His brow gathered in a deep frown, but he said not a word to her. Instead, he gave her the oddest look and rose to his feet to leave. With a few seconds he had crossed nearly their whole camp. It was that look and what she recognized it to mean that forced her to her feet to follow.

Disappointment shone from deep within him.

Disappointment in her.

Her stomach gripped and her heart pounded harder and louder in her chest. Her biggest fear now that her father summoned her back was that he would be disappointed in the woman she'd grown into. Already she knew she'd failed, but each additional example of her shortcomings said that she had so little to offer him. And that made her worry even more.

"Rurik," she called out. "Sir, wait."

Margriet hurried her steps to reach him and tugged at his arm to stop him from going farther away. He turned to her, but his eyes lowered to where her hand rested on his arm.

On the bare skin of his arm that grew hot beneath her touch.

And on the strong muscles beneath the bare skin.

Oh, my! Margriet released her hold, took a step back and waited for him to turn back to her before speaking.

"'Tis not that I am unwilling to do as you ask, sir. I am just not as familiar with the tongue as someone who teaches it need be."

"But, you have been speaking it easily with Sven," he said, in Norn. "You sound as comfortable with that as you do the Gaelic."

"It has been many years since I spoke either the common dialect or the formal court language. I spoke both when I was sent here ten years ago," she answered, switching back to the Gaelic she was more comfortable using. "Then I learned this one and have used it and no other daily at the convent."

Rurik laughed then, looking around at the rest of those still eating. "We have such a mongrel group here—a few who speak Gaelic, a few who speak Norn or the court tongue, a few who speak two, but only two of us speak all three."

Margriet realized the truth of his words, for only they spoke all three languages. Nodding in agreement, she wondered what to do. She had been speaking in Norn to Sven and Magnus and a couple of the other men, and it seemed that she fell back into it with each day they spent together. Of course, her father would expect her to use the correct language when she arrived, or at least when she made her appearance at the earl's court.

She'd learned that as a child. Having a father who served at the highest levels in the Orkneys and whose liege lord was a powerful man in both Sweden and Norway required using the words accepted at those levels. Earl Erengisl had been the former earl's closest advisor and even son-by-marriage when she'd left the islands and both he and her father had risen at the death of the last mormaer, Lord Maolise. So, of course, she would know how to speak at court.

Margriet remembered dimly a trip to the royal court in Norway just before her mother's death and even a visit to the lands that Lord Erengisl owned in the far-flung ends of Sweden. Nothing of the particulars remained in her memories, simply traveling with her mother and the grandeurs of those at court. Even a child could not fail to be impressed by the wealth and power of King Magnus's palace and courtiers.

Now, watching the expectation in his gaze, she decided to give him what he asked for. It would help her as well, for it would give her something to do during their hours on the road and it would sharpen her own skills, grown weak from lack of practice over the years. It could also help her fill in the gaps of her knowledge, true knowledge, of what had happened over the years she'd missed of her father's life. And that was a good thing.

"Aye," she said with a nod. "I will help you in this."

He smiled, and it was enough to make her heart stop. The warmth and approval of it shone brightly and Margriet thought that she had gifted him with his life's goal.

"My thanks, Sister." He looked around and called

to a few of the men—the Scots from the western highlands. "Leathen, Donald, Fergus," he said, pointing to each one as he named them, "Sister has agreed to teach you some Norn on our way north."

She nodded at each one and smiled. "I am glad to help you in this. Rurik tells me it is your wish to remain in the Orkneys?" she asked.

"Oh, aye," said Donald. "'Tis a chance to make our way in the world."

"Will you not miss your families?" Did they have no one to hold them in the Highlands?

"I have two older brothers to care for my parents," Leathen said. "My mother was pleased by Rurik's offer. She was despairing of me ever making a match in Lairig Dubh."

The other men laughed and one smacked Leathen on the shoulder. "No woman would have ye, Leathen."

"So, you all come from Lairig Dubh? Where is that?" she asked, glad to get the first clue about her guide and guard and hoping for more.

"Lairig Dubh is the home of the Clan MacLerie. 'Tis in the west of the Highlands, not far from Loch Lomond," Donald explained.

With his words, she realized right then that she would be able to learn more, not only about her father and the situation in the Orkneys and the Norse world, but also the background of the one chosen to bring her home. That thought grabbed her interest. He had only identified himself with the affiliation of that clan when he'd turned up at the convent's gates, looking as though he was from the north but calling himself with a clan name.

Who was he? Why did he live in Scotland, and not the north of it that used to belong to Norway, but deep in the heart of it? As though he sensed her interest in him, he met her gaze.

"You can begin on the morrow," Rurik explained, as he waved the men away. "Take turns through the day riding at her side," he called out.

"This will also work for Sister Elspeth," Margriet said. "She is from a local village and does not speak it, either."

"Ah," he said, crossing his arms of his chest and meeting her gaze, "but she and Sven are already teaching each other."

Margriet turned and looked for the two and discovered that they sat nearby and near each other, speaking back and forth in a low voice. Elspeth seemed to point to something and then give its name. Sven repeated the word, or stumbled over it in most tries, and soft laughter followed.

Her stomach twisted as the scene reminded her of her own behavior just a short few months ago with Finn. Words led to touches that led to passion that led to…disaster. She shook her head and faced Rurik.

"She is an innocent, Rurik. Order your man away."

"Of course she is, as are you, Sister."

His words startled her and so nearly exposed her own lack of innocence that she clamped her lips shut. He must have realized her surprise and he explained, "You are both nuns who have taken vows of chastity, so I assumed you were both innocents. Holy innocents."

Holy was not a word she would apply to herself, especially when she reacted solely as a woman to his raw masculinity. The tone of his voice sent heat through her body, but the words did not match the tone. And when her core pulsed deep within her and her breasts ached to be touched, it was difficult to connect the words to herself. Holy innocent? Elspeth, certainly, but not her.

"Does he understand?" she asked, nodding her head in the young couple's direction. This could bring disaster to their door too quickly.

'Twas only at the moment when their eyes met that she knew that he also recognized the danger in the arrangement. When she was of a mind, she could and would discover much more about him than he wished her to know. She watched as he followed the men and spoke quietly to them, most likely warning them to limit their discussions with her. She would need to have the same discussion with Elspeth over her past and the girl's to prepare for the questions that would come.

He approached now and nodded to Sven, who stood and assisted Elspeth to her feet. "'Tis getting late now, Sister, and there is a small village ahead on our path where I would like us to stop tomorrow eve. It will mean rising early and riding farther then we have so far, so a good night's rest will ready you for it."

He held out his hand, guiding her to a spot where they had arranged a tent between several trees. They walked silently then and Rurik lifted the flap so they could enter it. She watched as Elspeth crouched down and walked in and, when she turned to follow, he stopped her with a touch on her arm.

"My men," he began in Norn, "know what is expected of them in their behavior around you both. If any one of them is disrespectful or forward to you or to Sister Elspeth and I do not see it, tell me and I will make certain he learns how costly his failure is."

Margriet tried to swallow, but the ominous warning tightened her throat. She knew in that moment that she would never want to be the target of his anger.

"My thanks…" she began in Gaelic, and when he shook his head and glanced to where Elspeth had just entered, she knew he wished this to be between only them, so she continued in Norn as well. "My thanks for your concern, Rurik. No one had been anything but respectful to us."

He wanted her to say it again. He loved the way her tongue rolled when she said his name. Or sometimes it came out like a growl. He cared not how she said it, just that she did. Rurik found himself nodding at her words, and at the same time, being completely and thoroughly guilty of the very sin he promised that none of his men would commit.

"Rurik?"

There! She'd repeated it. He imagined ripping off

that damned veil and tangling his hands in the waves of her hair while plundering that ripe red mouth. As his body responded to his escalating desire, he shifted and crossed his arms to keep from grabbing her. Then he realized that he was lost in the fog of lust and she was asking him a question!

"Sister?" he replied, trying to force that crucial bit of knowledge into his mind. "Forgive me, my thoughts wandered for a moment," he offered in apology. Bringing his attention back to the matter under discussion, and knowing he was the worst culprit, he asked, "What was your question?"

"'Tis my turn to beg a boon from you, sir."

Rurik's eyes closed against his will and the image that swam before them was one of her begging…for very sinful things. He cleared his throat and opened his eyes. "A boon, Sister? What do you have need of?"

His body, especially his lower body, shuddered in anticipation and though he knew the request was something mundane, desire pushed forward hoping for something else. By Odin's Word, he needed to get himself under control or he would be a danger to her and to himself!

"I would like to talk with you, also, as we travel. I have many questions about my father and Lord Erengisl and how things are now in Kirkvaw and in Norway. I have been away for so long and received only an occasional letter from my father." She paused and looked deeply into his eyes. "And it has never been enough."

Rurik knew she had just revealed something personal and painful to him. His exile had been of his choosing, but hers, as was the situation with many daughters or wives, was not.

"Sven or Magnus would be better to ask those questions for I have not been in Kirkvaw for nigh on thirteen years now."

She gasped and her eyes blinked rapidly at his disclosure. Rurik had surprised himself, for he did not intend for her to know that much about himself. But, he felt the pain she carried over her abandonment and offered it as a salve on the wounds.

"Thirteen years? You have lived in Scotland for thirteen years?"

"Aye, longer than you, but not by much more."

"You were much older than I was when I arrived here."

He could see that she was warming to ask more questions and wanted to stop her. Aye, he'd opened the matter with his admission, but he wanted it to go no further than that. There were questions he did not want to answer to himself, let alone to her, so he put her off about them.

"Aye and much older even now, Sister. Here now," he said, lifting the side of the tent so she could enter, "the morning will be here too soon and you need to rest."

The flash of pain in her eyes nearly stopped him, for he knew his dismissal was a curt one. He fought not to back down from his stance, for there was much danger in doing so. Still, he'd felt the pain of exile and could not stop himself from trying to soften the blow.

"We have many days yet ahead of us on the rest of the journey for your questions," he added, sounding much less concerned than he was.

The shadow of her pain still reflected within her eyes, but she nodded in agreement and went inside without further argument or comment. Rurik's heart pounded, for hurting her was never his intention and he wanted to see her smile at him instead of wincing from the pain of rejection.

Had she any notion of how much alike their stories were? Both in exile from family and friends. Both recalled for honor and duty's sake. Both resisting that call.

Rurik stepped back and let the canvas flap drop to close the women inside. No matter how much he wanted to hold her and comfort her, their differences were what mattered now.

For he was a man and she a woman.

For he was Erengisl's son and she was Gunnar's daughter.

For he was a bastard warrior about to masquerade as a honorable man and she was… What?

Rurik knew it to deep in his bones that she was not a nun. He could not prove it, but the feeling was too strong to be wrong. Margriet did not wear the habit and veil as a sign of holy vows. He just did not know why she did, but he would discover her secret before the journey's end. The problem and dangers lay in that he both carried secrets and protected them. As he was certain she did.

While he walked once more around the perimeter of their camp, he wondered about hers. Things had changed much in the last ten years, the situation made more tenuous by the death of Lord Maolise and the assumption of his own father to the position of the Earl of the Orkneys, a title not inherited, but more taken through marriage. Now, trouble between the king and his sons forced Erengisl's hand and brought his own return to the Orkneys.

Rurik nodded to the guards as he circled once more. He did his best thinking while pacing or walking, so he continued trying to decide how Margriet fit in to all this. Was it just coincidental that they returned at the same time? Was his task to escort her home simply an efficient means of getting her from the convent?

And what bond would her father cement with her hand in marriage? For marriage agreements were the basis of everything—the underlying connections between families, between friends, between enemies. Did Gunnar plan that Margriet would be a gift to a friend or would seal a bargain to end enmity between two rival families?

No matter which scenario, Gunnar would not stand by as his daughter entered the convent. And neither was this woman for him, nor he for her. Their destinies were entwined during this journey, but would part and go in entirely different directions when they arrived. 'Twas even likely they would not see each other again after this journey was completed.

So for now, he would learn about her and the secrets she carried, all the while trying to protect his own. The pain he witnessed in her gaze when he shunned her only brought back his own memories of the same and he had no wish to feel that once more. Rurik would wait until he heard the offer from his father's own lips before believing it and accepting it.

For now, he was still his own man.

Later? Only the Almighty knew.

Chapter Nine

The sun had barely peeked over the horizon when the call came to wake and be about the day. Thinking this was worse than the convent's schedule, Margriet carried out her morning routine, chewing her herbs and sipping water, and then roused Elspeth from sleep. The girl slept from the time she lay her head down until the time her name was called, but there had been no sleep for Margriet this night.

Trying to stretch out the soreness in her back that must have been the cause of her sleeplessness, Margriet tucked her braid inside her tunic and placed the veil and wimple back over her hair. She hated it more with each passing day—the rough fabric that surrounded her face and neck and the prickly, long veil that added weight and caught her hair with every movement.

Complaining about something she'd brought on herself made no sense, so Margriet crawled from the tent and stood up in the cool morning air. Upon seeing Donald was their guard, she greeted him in Gaelic and then repeated it in Norn, asking him to do the same. He smiled and tried to imitate her pronunciation, but with comical results. The good thing was that he had tried and she had no doubt he would improve with practice.

Once Elspeth joined them, Donald led them down a path to the edge of the river, though now not much more than a stream, and gave them a measure of privacy as they washed and took care of other needs. Margriet only dared loosen the strap of the wimple a bit to dab water on her neck and face.

Watching as Elspeth did the same, she realized the sacrifices that the young woman was making on her behalf. Although Elspeth had excitedly agreed to her plan, for it gave her a chance to leave the convent and a future of prayer behind, it had not so far produced anything promised to her in return. When they arrived at her father's house and had straightened out all of the misunderstandings and mistakes, Margriet would make it worthwhile for the girl. A call from the camp drew them back for a hasty meal of porridge and weak ale and then they were riding north.

This day, the sun decided to hide behind the clouds and the air took a cold turn, with the winds picking up steadily as they traveled toward the coast. Time moved faster, or so 'twould seem, but Margriet knew it was just that speaking to the three Scots and teaching them words and phrases in Norn helped it pass by more quickly. They stopped two or three times for comfort, but Rurik pushed them a bit harder, as he'd promised the night before.

As the sun dropped down lower into the sky, they met up with the man Rurik always sent ahead to secure their nighttime camp. Word spread through the column of riders that they would sleep indoors this night. Margriet smiled at the very thought of a bed beneath her. Even a thin pallet would be a gluttony of comfort after so many nights on the hard ground with only a blanket or two between them.

Leaning over, she whispered words of warning to Elspeth about their behavior in this village. They'd become lax in their pretenses and they needed to have a care lest they be exposed for their lies. After years of living in the convent, they would simply need to imitate the nuns' prayerful ways a bit more while being watched.

The men seemed just as excited as she was to approach a village, but they gathered closer to her and Elspeth as though danger was near. Finally, just before the sun set, they arrived at the village.

Built up in the place where the river they'd been following north met up with another that headed west and deeper into Caithness and then onto Scotland, it was a rambling gathering of wooden houses and a few shops and an inn that could not be confused with the bustling Kirkvaw or even the smaller Thurso or Wick. She spied no church and no convent as they rode up to a squat, two-story inn on the outer edge of the rest of the village.

The innkeeper, a man nearly as wide as he was tall and who must have smelled the coin to be had from a group of travelers such as theirs, rolled out of the doorway and approached them. A few other men and two young women peeked out of windows to watch the goings-on. The women loosened their bodices in a display that was as vulgar as it was unnecessary, for after days on a journey with only two nuns and the limitations that their calling meant, the men in the group did not miss those of the fairer sex. Even whorish ones, who nearly tumbled out the windows while offering their wares without shame.

At Rurik's signal, no one dismounted. Donald and Leathen even took hold of the reins of her horse and Elspeth's as though readying themselves for flight. The tension had grown steadily, filling the air around them as Rurik negotiated their accommodations, food and other items they needed for their journey.

Only when he nodded and grasped the innkeeper's arm in agreement did the men climb from their horses and release their hold of their weapons. When the two women sauntered out into the yard, both barefoot with their hair hanging uncovered and loose down their backs and their bosoms falling out of their bodices with the same abandon, Margriet found herself forgotten atop her horse. Watching the lustful expressions on the men and seeing them jostle to get a better view of what was being offered for sale, she knew that coin was not the only thing that would be spread this night in the village.

A noise caught her attention and she turned to find Sven helping Elspeth from her mount and waiting for her to steady on her feet before letting go of his hold around her waist. Just when she was about to speak, Rurik approached and reached for her. Sven stepped away from Elspeth, but not before sharing some meaningful look with the girl.

She slid down from the horse, guided to her feet by Rurik, as the innkeeper came closer. He bowed his head and nodded several times, never meeting her gaze, as Rurik explained that they would spend the night here. Rurik called out several orders and she found herself escorted inside by Harald, as he was called. The women disappeared and she dared not ask where they went.

Margriet ducked her head to pass through the doorway and found the inn was divided into two sections, a large room to the right where a hearth almost filled one wall and a smaller chamber that aromas told her was a kitchen. The larger room had a collection of mismatched tables and benches spread around it and she and Elspeth were led there to sit.

Worried about her reaction to the young women, Margriet was pleased when an older woman carried out a tray of sizzling meats that were surrounded by some cooked turnips and a pool of juices. Her mouth watered at the sight and especially at the smells, since they'd eaten only stews and soups on the journey. The second trip brought steaming loaves of bread, coarse and brown, like that served in the convent, and a clay pot of butter. The other women only appeared when the innkeeper called for ale to be served.

On closer inspection—and Margriet admitted to herself that she was curious—the two were older than they appeared from a distance. Although they enticed and teased with their copious amounts of naked flesh, they had apparently never heard anyone like Mother Ingrid and her lecture on cleanliness. It mattered not to any of the men, for every time they poured ale or leaned over nearer the table, the men's tongues almost touched the floor.

The only one not falling under their spell was Rurik.

He sat in a chair, at the table next to hers, and watched everything without saying a word. A nod at one or another brought their behavior under control, or it did until the laces of the brown-haired one's blouse finally gave way under the weight of her heavy breasts and one of those breasts fell out of its covering. Margriet blinked and then blinked again, trying to ignore the men's feverish noises and never dreaming that someone would be so bold in the presence of two nuns, real or not.

Rurik gathered himself as though to rise when Harald yelled at the woman in a loud voice. A mutinous and pouting lower lip quivered for a moment before the woman, Ragna as she was called, lifted the breast and slid it back inside her clothing, tying the laces slowly as every male in the room watched. The knot did not catch the first time and Ragna slid her hand over the nipple this time, gasping as though surprised that it hardened beneath her touch. Margriet was certain every man's rod did the same as they watched the display.

Margriet looked away, now embarrassed beyond measure, as did Elspeth. Rurik waved the innkeeper over to stop this and Harald ran up to Ragna, grabbed her and flung her across the room, toward the door. She stumbled out the door and they could hear the angry words followed by a hard slap and then silence. Furious whispering continued for several minutes and then the door opened. Now fully covered and with her laces secured, Ragna walked back into the room, lifted the pitcher she'd left on the table and began serving ale once more.

Chastened, her cheek reddened from Harald's blow, the woman was not blatant in her invitations, but Margriet saw the looks she gave to a few of the men and knew several accepted the unspoken message. When she served Margriet and Elspeth, the ale splashed over the cup and Ragna backed up to clean it up, placing her also-ample bottom right in front of Rurik's face. The other one, with wild red hair and a bosom that matched Ragna's, must have been worried that he would choose her rival, for she rushed to his side, bending down to make certain he could see all the way down to her waist, too.

Whores were a fact of life, but to be confronted in this manner, when she could not respond as a noblewoman should, made Margriet angry. Thinking back on Rurik's words, she wondered if this was the reason for their stay in the village. She turned to find Rurik staring at her. Looking at the women and then back at her, he motioned for them to lean closer.

The pig! How could he pay attention to them and all they offered right before her? Did he not know that his behavior gave his men the same right to do so in front of them? Before she could explode in outrage, the two women faced her and murmured words of apology to her and Elspeth.

Choking on the words that were fighting their way out, Margriet tore off a piece of bread, dipped it into the venison juice on her plate and stuffed it in her mouth. She chewed and chewed, trying to soften the bread so it could be swallowed, but it would not move off her tongue. The cup appeared in her hands just as she could feel a cough build in her chest and throat. The mouthful of ale finally helped her clear the dry bread.

When she looked over at Elspeth, she was so red, Margriet thought her fevered. Sliding her arm under the girl's, she stood, taking Elspeth with her. No one stopped them, but once outside in the cool air of the evening, she discovered Sven a few paces behind them.

"We needed some air, Sven. Do not think to stop us," Margriet began. Other words, bad ones, formed in her thoughts, but she stopped them before she could say them. None were suitable for a nun to be thinking, let alone saying aloud.

Not pausing to look back or forward, she dragged Elspeth with her away from the inn. She could hear

Sven's heavy steps behind them, most likely following to protect them, although in her mind, the bigger danger lay within the room they'd left. Margriet continued at her fast pace until she felt Elspeth lag at her side. Releasing her and knowing that Sven would stop with her, Margriet looked up and decided to walk to the stream they'd followed into this godforsaken village.

Mayhap she would even walk back to the convent and stay there!

She had no idea of how much time had passed or how much distance she covered, but now the sun was gone and the birds of night were calling out their warning. There was enough moonlight to see around her and she found a large rock to sit on while her temper cooled.

This was exactly what she feared when she donned the nun's habit for protection. Men who lost control when faced with the least bit of provocation. Men who behaved like pigs, rooting for their pleasure. Margriet kicked a few smaller stones into the stream as her anger pulsed through her. She was so wrapped within it, she almost did not hear him approach.

Almost.

He stood a few paces behind her and said nothing. Probably for want of words, for what could be said? She leaned down and picked up another handful of pebbles, tossing each one as far as she could into the water and hearing them plop on the surface.

"I worried that you might have fallen in the water," he said softly.

Margriet would credit him on his approach, for he avoided all the sticky subjects and chose a more humorous one. Of course 'twas only humorous if she admitted to lying about that event.

"I tripped," she said, not yet willing to admit anything to this man whose face had lately been looking down a whore's gown.

Tossing another of her pebbles into the stream, she slid off the rock, dusted the dirt from the habit and walked to the edge of the rushing stream. Though she could be mistaken, it appeared to be shallow, but the light of the moon was not enough to tell truly and accurately. Footsteps behind her warned that he was coming nearer.

"Do you feel the need to trip now? Again?" he asked, his voice coming over her left shoulder. She'd thought him farther away.

Margriet released the rest of the stones from her hand and sighed. "'Tis colder than that night."

"Ah, so you only trip when the air is hot then?"

His words were like a caress to her, drifting softly and slowly around her, lulling her into letting down her guard. The night birds sang in the trees behind them, although she recognized none of the songs. The land and its creatures were different the farther north they traveled, away from all that was familiar and safe to her.

"Aye, 'tis then that the danger of falling is greater,"

she said, playing along with the lie. Then, it was over and she needed to say some of the words bubbling inside. She needed to ask the questions that plagued her the most. "Do they not know that it is a sin?"

"Do you mean the men or the women?" he asked with no levity in his voice. "Is temptation the sin or is it only when we give in to it and commit the trespass?"

Margriet turned now to look at him, not trusting her judgment that he did not jest in his question. His face, outlined by moonbeams, appeared stern and serious, but she had the deep sensation that this was a different side of him than he showed to most. Recalling the lessons of the convent, ones she'd failed in the last few months, she repeated Mother Ingrid's words to him.

"If temptation is offered apurpose to draw someone in to sin, then the tempter sins as well as the one who falls."

He leaned in closer and whispered, "And if the tempter knows not what they do?"

Memories assailed her, images of Finn and his soft words and touches that drew her along a path to her own sin. Now thinking on it, she behaved with him the same way the men behaved with the harlots at the inn. He enticed her, making her want more, making her want things she did not know possible between a man and woman, things best kept from innocents with no defenses. Then he taught her to respond to his call, whether it was his touch or his voice or the love he offered her.

Oh, aye, she'd fallen hard and fast into the sins of lust and fornication. Calling it love, calling it temptation, did not change its true nature…or her own. It was a sin and she'd trespassed greatly.

Tears gathered in her eyes and she blinked to hide them from him. This realization, how much alike she was to the men inside clamoring for what the women offered, and how much like the women, clamoring to give their virtue away, hurt deeply. She would be called "whore" when her condition was known, proving her sin to one and all.

"Sin is sin," she answered back, without the true conviction that a daughter of the church should have.

Did she know the temptation she offered, just by standing and speaking? With every movement of her hands or every step she took, she called to something inside him, something that should know better than to answer. But answer it did, and the desire for her grew with each day.

His plan to befriend her failed only moments after he'd decided upon it. His years of appreciating women, and all they offered, had taken his control and crushed it cruelly, making him consider that it was an apparition and never truly there at all. Rurik did not know which was worse, which more a threat to him and to her—the enticement of her flashing eyes, soft bow mouth and womanly curves, or the pain that lashed through her now.

When she lifted her head and he caught sight of the tears that filled her eyes, he searched them for the truth—what could Gunnar's daughter know of sin? Her life, at least the part of her life when her conduct was her own, had been in a convent, sheltered from the worst life had to offer. Yet, pain seeped into her voice as she spoke and into every part of her that he could behold.

Rurik felt his own pain well up inside him. The rejection by his father and the insult to his mother's honor brought about by his birth and their life stung and made him recognize something in her gaze. Something he wanted to ease and to soothe and to warn away. He forgot himself in that moment. He forgot what she was and all the reasons why he should not touch her.

He leaned down to touch his lips to hers, just as he'd been craving to do since the first time he'd glimpsed her beauty and felt the desire rise within him. Rurik slid his finger under her chin and tilted hers higher so that he could taste the mouth that drew him in.

"Temptation is temptation, Rurik," she whispered.

He heard the words and felt them, too, since his lips were nearly touching hers now. Then her hand slid up and pressed against his chest, stopping him from moving that last fraction of distance between them. He ached to taste her now, especially now that he could feel her breath on his face and smell the scent that was hers alone. His manhood swelled and he shifted closer to her as his whole body throbbed in readiness.

And then he did taste her lips and he felt her surprise as he touched his lips to those that bedeviled him in his sleep and all his waking hours, too. If she had pulled back, Rurik would have stopped himself, but when she pressed against him, he slid his tongue along her lips until she opened to him. He released his hold on her chin and slid his hands down to grasp her shoulders—steadying him or her he knew not. He only knew that she was as delectable and enticing as he suspected she would be.

Rurik tilted his head and covered her mouth completely with his, dipping his tongue now in the heat of it, hearing and feeling her gasp as he continued his invasion. Not willing to retreat or relent, he played now with her tongue, drawing it forward and sucking on it gently. Margriet softened against him, and he took it for permission to deepen the kiss.

Using every bit of persuasion he'd ever learned in loving women, Rurik teased her mouth while he pulled her closer. Lifting his mouth only long enough to draw in a ragged breath and to allow her one, he possessed her once more…and then again…and again. He reached up slowly, not willing to disturb the growing passion, and slipped his hand under her veil. Tangling in her hair, he began to unravel the braids he found, when she suddenly stepped from his embrace.

Rurik met her desire-filled gaze and smiled at her, reeling from the very taste and scent of her. Margriet shook her head and looked away.

"I cannot."

The words, spoken almost too low to be heard, were

like a battle cry to his ears. Her words had vibrated against his lips before, but this time he heard them and they were words he could not ignore. As if to confirm that this was unseemly at the least and sacrilege at the worst, Sven's voice called out through the silence. Her hand remained on his chest until that moment, when she reached up and touched her lips.

Sven broke through the trees and whether 'twas Rurik's action or hers, Rurik stepped away from Margriet so quickly that she stumbled. When he reached out to steady her, his hand slipped, knocking her away. Putting some distance between them was a good thing, but what was not was that Margriet stood on the edge of the stream. His slight push was enough to send her stumbling off balance and off the uneven ground and into the water.

Sven yelled.

Rurik yelled louder.

And Margriet screamed as the icy water sucked her down under its surface.

Chapter Ten

When he grabbed for her, all he could reach was the end of her habit, which tore as he held it fast. A glimpse of naked legs was more than the situation needed at this moment and Rurik cursed under his breath as Margriet flailed about in the water.

Sven arrived at his side and Rurik unbuckled his scabbard and jumped into the water after her. The stream's current was much stronger than it appeared from the edge and he found that it moved both of them rapidly away from where Sven stood, his mouth agape, watching them as they floated downstream.

It took some effort, but Rurik was finally able to take ahold of Margriet and plant his feet in a shallow enough place to stop them from moving farther away. The darkness made it more difficult to judge how and where to move. And so did Margriet's struggles against the water, her heavy clothing and his hold.

"Stay still or I will lose my grasp," he warned, waiting for his men to reach them.

"You pushed me!" she accused as she also fought the wimple and veil that now covered most of her face.

"You slipped," he said through clenched jaws.

They were surrounded by help just then so her arguing ceased. He handed her across to Sven and Magnus, who pulled her out of the water. Standing on the bank as he climbed out, she looked like an old dog dragged in from a storm. Margriet glared at him, an action ruined by the chattering teeth and shivering of her body in reaction to the very cold water and the cool night's air.

"Sister," Donald said, "what happened to you?" He took a blanket one of the others held out and tossed it around her shoulders.

"I slipped."

"She slipped."

They offered the explanation at the same time and, if the vehemence of it belied the truth, no one said a thing to dispute their words. Looking from one to another of his men, Rurik knew some had their doubts about what had happened when he followed the nuns from the inn and only one returned with Sven.

"Sven? Sister Elspeth?" he asked, drawing attention to something other than this.

"She is safely back at the inn. Harald made ready the upstairs room for the sisters as you asked and promised to send up food when Sister Margriet returns."

They began walking back toward the inn and, when Margriet stumbled over the edges of her sodden tunic and gown for the third time, he stopped, scooped her up into his arms and continued on. The one good thing that their dunking had done was cool his ardor at the moment. Any inkling of it returning was continually doused by the stream of icy water pouring down over the lower half of his body from her garments with each step he took.

When they arrived back at the inn, the men had finished eating and most were readying for sleep. The tables were pushed to the walls of the room, the benches turned over on top of them, and blankets were being spread as each man picked a spot on the packed dirt floor. Rurik quickly checked to see if all were present and noted that two men were not. He did not have to ask Sven where they were, he only hoped that the nuns did not notice.

Now following Harald, Rurik carried Margriet up the stairs and down the short hallway to the sleeping room that she would share with Sister Elspeth. The younger nun stood waiting just inside by the door, while Heinrek guarded in the hallway. When he placed Margriet on her feet, Sister Elspeth waved them out of the room and tended to her alone.

Thankfulness for his escape from the chamber lasted only until he saw the expressions on Sven's and Magnus's faces. 'Twas obvious what they were thinking and Rurik was tempted to disabuse them by force. Then he thought better of it. He accepted his scabbard back and after settling it back on his hips, he crossed his arms over his chest in a challenge to them to question his word and honor—if they dared.

He offered only one explanation to them as he pushed past them to go downstairs and make arrangements for the nuns' comfort.

"She slipped."

The silence grew behind him and Rurik thought his escape good until Sven's whisper reached him.

"Puir wee woman."

Puir wee woman indeed, he thought as he went to see to her food. He found Harald's wife hurrying around the kitchen, gathering bread, meat, some cheese and broth onto a tray to take to the sisters. The other two women were, as he expected, not to be seen, although in the scattered moments of quiet as he watched the preparations, they *could* be heard.

"Sister Margriet will have need of a sewing needle and thread to repair her garments," he mentioned.

"I will do that," Thora offered. "'Tis the least I can do for her after the way Ragna and Morag chased them out with their brazen ways." Thora threw a look at Harald, who bowed his head and said not a thing in reply. However, he wore the appearance of a man thoroughly chastened for his misdeeds.

Rurik followed Thora back to the chamber and waited while she delivered the tray within. He could hear the women exchanging words, but could not make out what was being said. Soon, the door opened and Thora stepped out carrying the habit in her hands, making certain to hold it away from herself as it still dripped. She talked under her breath as she left, connecting names, fates and a few curses, too. Another set of clothing that matched the wet one in color and texture—but this one dry—was tucked under her arm.

"I promised the holy sisters that I would wash and repair their garments as penance for what they were forced to see here," Thora said, while blessing herself with her free hand. "What is your penance for allowing it?" she asked, passing him by without waiting for his answer.

The woman had no idea of the price he was paying for what had happened. His punishment was indeed a high price, for it was the realization that there was a woman he could want and not have. Rurik shook his head as he waved Heinrek away and took up a position near the door. He would take a watch tonight, sleeping outside their door to make certain nothing untoward happened. Well, nothing *else* untoward.

Rurik knocked softly on the door and waited for their response. 'Twas Sister Elspeth who answered his call.

"Have you need of anything else, Sister?"

"No, sir."

"Is Sister Margriet well?" Rurik leaned his head against the door as he asked, thinking once more of what had happened and what had almost happened between them this night.

"She is, sir."

"Until morn then," he said. He waited for any

other word or sound, but when none came, Rurik stepped away and took a stance between their door and the hallway.

He heard some movement over the next half of an hour within the chamber, but nothing spoken. Then, those inside quieted and he knew they were abed. Sliding down against the wall, he sat on the floor and waited in the darkened corridor for night to pass.

Sometime later—Rurik was not certain how much time had passed—he heard the soft sound of a woman crying. It hurt to hear it, especially since he knew it was Margriet. He accepted the pain as another part of his penance this night. When it ceased and the room grew quiet once more, he climbed to his feet and went to the door.

After listening for any sounds inside, he lifted the latch quietly and opened the door a crack. The faint light from a slow-burning tallow lamp threw shadows across the room, but it was enough for him to see around the room.

Two shapes lay side by side in the bed, neither moving as he crept in and walked to the side of it. Sister Elspeth slept in a huddled lump, blankets pulled up so that only the top of her head was visible above them. Margriet slept with wild abandon.

Her blanket was thrown back, exposing the chemise she wore as nightclothes. She slept with one leg under the blankets and the other uncovered. Her hair, now dry and laying in waves of curls about her head, caught the light of the candle and seemed to be a gathering of the darkest storm clouds around her face. As Rurik stepped closer, he noticed the tracks of tears marring her cheeks.

Torn between simply watching her sleep and waking her to beg her forgiveness for his near-assault, the sigh that escaped her caught him by surprise. He stood completely still as she mumbled words under her breath and turned on her side toward him. Tucking one hand under her head, she settled back into a deeper sleep.

The chamber quieted again with Sister Elspeth's soft snoring the only noise now. Rurik checked the small hearth and added a few more blocks of peat to add some warmth to the room. He checked the small windows to see that the shutters were secured against the wind that was building outside and then walked to the door. With a final look at Margriet, he left and took his place outside the door for the rest of the night.

A knock on the door woke her, but Margriet hesitated to answer it. From the light that forced its way in around the wooden shutters on the windows, she could tell the sun had risen some time ago. Wondering at the laziness of her escorts, she pushed back her blankets and crept to the door. The knock came again, but this time Thora called her name softly. Tugging one of the blankets free, she gathered her hair and tucked it under her chemise as she wrapped the length of wool around her shoulders.

She lifted the latch and opened the door to find the

innkeeper's wife standing with her hands filled. Taking the tray from her, Margriet stood back and allowed her inside. Leaning over, she peered into the hallway, looking for Rurik and not finding him. Thora laid the two gowns and tunics over a bench and then turned to Margriet.

"*He said* to ready yerselves for the day. *He said* he wants to leave wi'in the hour." Thora snorted then to let Margriet know exactly what the woman thought about *him*.

"My thanks for your work on this," Margriet said as she lifted her gown and inspected the neat sewing that reattached the seam where it had split apart. "And for putting more peat on the fire during the night. I felt the chill, but could not rouse myself to get out of bed to do that." She pulled the blanket tightly around her shoulders.

Thora stared at her and shook her head. "I didna do any such thing. *He* ordered us away from the stairs and e'en took a place outside yer door to make certain ye werena disturbed."

Margriet looked at the open door and wondered if Rurik had stirred the fire in the dark of the night to keep them warm. Before she could think on it, Thora approached.

"If ye dinna mind me asking, Sister?" When Margriet did not object, Thora went on. "Why is it that two holy sisters—" she paused then to make the sign of the cross and bow her head "—travel with such a man?"

Margriet sighed. "My father calls me home and Rurik was sent to escort me."

"He is a strong one, he is, and ye willna have to worry aboot yer safety wi' him guarding ye. But, I have never heard of holy sisters—" another pause, another sign of the cross "—traveling with a group of men."

Elspeth stirred as they talked and Margriet wanted this over. "My father vouched for his worthiness," she began and was met with a stare of frank disbelief. "He gave me no choice and there was no time to send word to my father over the matter." Again, Thora blinked as though she'd never heard of such a thing… and well, neither had Margriet.

"He is my cousin. Kin from my mother's family," she lied when all other attempts to explain failed.

"Ah," Thora said, nodding in acceptance. "Kin then?" Thora walked to the door and then turned back. "I wi' tell *him* ye are getting ready."

Elspeth began to push back the blankets and stopped as she realized they were not alone. Margriet nodded at the woman and watched her leave, lowering the latch to keep the door shut. Elspeth climbed from the bed and immediately began searching the tray for food. 'Twas then that Margriet realized her stomach did not churn as it did in the morn. Afraid not to use the herbs and to get sick once they were on the road, she sniffed at the food to see if it caused the ailment to begin.

All she smelled was fresh bread and some cold meats. Could she be past the worst of it as the cook had explained?

"You are not green, Lady Margriet," Elspeth commented. "How do you feel? Are you hungry?" The girl began eating, but Margriet hesitated.

She'd only eaten some bread dipped in hot broth before sleeping last eve, abstaining from the venison roast after her return. By now, she would be heaving. Instead, she could feel a growing appetite within her. Worried that the sickness might return later, she tucked her herbs into the pocket of her tunic as she dressed. Better to be prepared then caught off guard.

It did not take even close to an hour for them to dress and eat, and soon she and Elspeth walked down the steps to the common room where she knew the men had slept. The tables and benches were filled with men breaking their fast, but Margriet did not pause there for fear of seeing the round-heeled wenches again. That sight would ruin her day before it began.

Walking outside, the winds buffeted against them. Cooler by much than the day before, Margriet made certain her wimple and veil were secured. Sven greeted them in Gaelic, which brought a smile to Elspeth's face. The girl, in turn, tried to say the same words in Norn to him and Margriet watched as his expression softened at her attempt.

This was not good. Although she doubted Elspeth would expose their secret, encouraging a relationship between this commoner girl and this nobleman's son was like building a fire in the middle of the dry season—it would burn hot and destroy everything in its path. Still, putting obstacles in their way would only heighten the interest between them.

So long as Sven respected the boundaries between him and "Sister" Elspeth, there was no harm in them speaking to each other. Margriet planned to keep watch over them and warn Rurik if things got out of hand. The absurdity of that thought struck her as she approached that very same man.

He stood with his back to them, tightening the straps of his saddle in place. He stopped for a moment and bowed his head. Margriet thought he might even be praying, until he shook his head and muttered something under his breath that sounded like some oath to a pagan god. Straightening up, he turned and saw them.

He looked horrible! At first glance, she thought him ill, for he had lost his robust bearing and seemed instead to be weighted down. Margriet fought the urge to go to him, to touch his cheek, to fix whatever ailed him. It was only Elspeth's cough that brought her to her senses in time to avoid a very unseemly display.

"Good morrow, sisters," he said in greeting.

"Good morrow, sir," Elspeth said in return as she passed him. Sven led her to her horse and waited to help her mount.

"Good morrow, Rurik," Margriet said, unable to stop from saying his name. Her lips tingled as she spoke it, much as they had last eve when he kissed her. Now, he stood aside as Heinrek helped her into her seat atop the horse.

She watched now as the rest of the men stumbled out of the inn and into the light of day. Many looked as though they'd slept little and not well at all. 'Twas when several would not meet her gaze that she comprehended the problem, though knowing of it and knowing how to handle it were two different matters.

They had paid for the harlots' attentions.

Confused over how she felt and how she should react, Margriet focused her thoughts on the church's teachings on fornication. She felt the heat of embarrassment creep up into her cheeks as one of them did offer a greeting. She knew what they'd done—something a "holy innocent," as Rurik called them, should have no knowledge of the act or even understand any but the sketchiest of specifics about it.

But Margriet knew the pleasure of a man's touch, the thrill of joining her body to another's, and the wonderment of the act of giving herself to the man she loved. Although the harlots did not give themselves for the purest of reasons, no purity was involved at all, Margriet did not doubt that they enjoyed plying their wares and the coin it brought them. So, she found it a thorny matter to see their faces and know *what* they'd done in the darkest part of the night.

Margriet decided that avoidance was her best path for now and she bowed her head, trying to appear in prayer. Mayhap they would think it to be for the forgiveness of their immortal souls? Her attempt was interrupted by Rurik. Acting as though he was adjusting the strap of her stirrups and saddle, he waved the group forward under Magnus's lead.

"I would speak to you for a moment, Sister."

Something was wrong, for he did not hesitate this time in calling her that. He always hesitated. He held the reins of her horse now, so she had no way of avoiding this.

"I have wronged you and would ask your pardon," he said without meeting her gaze. "Especially for my behavior last night."

He did look up now, but when she saw the pain there, she wished he had not. "Rurik," she began, but she stopped as he continued.

"Nay, let me say this, I beg you." He waited for her to allow him and then he did. "I have lived the last thirteen years seeking pleasure where it may be, and have never met a woman I wanted who I could not have." He offered a sad smile. "Until you."

Margriet did not know whether to be pleased or insulted by his admission. She was no common girl like those at the inn to be ogled and desired, but a part of her was flattered.

"I should not have allowed you to even be in the same place last night with those women. You should not have had to endure their antics or even their presence."

"I have met fallen women before, Rurik," she began to explain, somehow wanting to ease whatever guilt he felt. Especially since she was not the holy innocent he thought her to be.

"Nay, Sister," he said, stopping her from saying anything else. "'Tis my fault. As is…"

"Please, Rurik, do not speak of it," she interrupted. "Nothing happened between us. Nothing," she assured him.

He felt vaguely insulted by her declaration instead of comforted by it, but he did not argue this time. He nodded and then mounted his horse. With a tug on the reins of her horse, he guided her forward to follow the rest, now a few dozen yards ahead of them.

Of course, she was lying, for he could see it in her eyes when she spoke. Something important had happened between them and his denial or hers would not change a moment of it in his memory. They may have spoken about the temptation offered by the harlots to the other men, but he spoke of the temptation between he and her. And the kiss that happened was simply a sign of how strong that temptation was growing to be.

He offered up a prayer that the rest of the journey would go swiftly, for Rurik did not know if he could count on his self-control when it came to her any longer.

By mid-morning, he knew things were not going to go as easily as he'd prayed they go. The sun had not yet climbed to its highest place in the sky when disaster struck and, by the time it did just after noon, only three of them remained upright—he, Sven and Sister Margriet.

Chapter Eleven

"Do you think it's plague?" Rurik asked. He feared saying the very word, but he needed to know what they were fighting, or not.

"Nay," she said shaking her head. "There are no buboes or other signs of plague among them. I fear they ate something bad."

Sister Margriet, as he now forced himself to think of her, turned and looked at the group of men and one woman, who lay on blankets in the shaded place beneath the only copse of trees he could get them to. They'd left the village and rode out onto the flatlands that typified most of Caithness as it approached the coast. Bogs and marshlands for miles and miles, with nary a hill or rising anywhere.

"Bad food?" Sven asked. "But we all ate at the inn last night and this morning. Why are we three yet spared from this?" Sven shook his head and then met his gaze. "Or will we yet be struck down as they are?"

"Do you think they were poisoned then?" she asked. "If this were contagion, we would be sick or beginning to be, but we are not." She placed her hands on her hips in a challenge to be proven wrong. Before he could offer his thoughts on the matter, she waggled a finger in their faces. "I have seen this before, at the convent, when tainted beef was given as a gift to the community there. Everyone who ate it spent two days wishing they were dead and this appears to be the same."

She'd surprised him with her strength as the crisis happened. One by one, his men and then Sister Elspeth grew ill, first with the stomach ailment and now, the other. Rurik had gotten them off the road, and built a rough shelter while Sister Margriet and Sven tended to the sick. Sven seemed to spend most of his time and efforts tending to *one* of the sick, but Sister Margriet soon dragged him away to tend to the others.

"Do you think they caught your stomach ailment?" Sven asked. "Though you seemed to have recovered from that."

Sister Margriet choked before she could say a word and Rurik reached out to steady her on her feet before she fell over. "Nay, this is not the same," she finally said.

Rurik had no experience treating the sick or even being sick, so he waited for her to decide their course in this. When she did not, he prodded her on. "What should we do then? Surely, they cannot continue in this manner—" he grimaced at the sounds around him "—for much longer?"

"First, whatever they ate that was tainted must pass through their bodies," she said. Sven now met his glance with a grimace of his own. "The most important thing is to get fluid into them."

"But they keep losing it," Sven pointed out as several of the men did just that.

"I have something that could help settle their stomachs while the rest…moves through." Sister Margriet reached into the pocket of her tunic and took out a small packet.

Rurik felt sick even if he did not have the same ailment as those around them. "What is that?"

"I do not travel well," she began. He and Sven both nodded at her, remembering several times when that was not as complete a description as he would have used. "The cook at the convent gave me these." She opened the packet to reveal some crushed herbs. "If you can get me a pot of water and build a fire to heat it, I could make a potion for them to drink. It could help."

It struck him as a sound plan, so he took the cooking pot and rode off to the stream to get the water she required. When he returned, Sven had a fire blazing and, within a short time, her potion was brewing. Over the next few hours, she moved among the sick, urging, bribing, even threatening one and all to make them drink some of it. And then she began all over again.

Rurik could not help but watch her as she took control, ordering him and Sven to do her bidding as though running a household for her lord and husband. And do her bidding they did, as promptly and thoroughly as they could. She gave orders as easily as a commander on the field of battle, and her methods were as efficient as they were effective. Nothing—not time, not resources, not words—was wasted as they battled to save their band of travelers.

On the second day, she ordered him back to the village to get supplies for them. Her instructions were clear and concise, down to the amount of flour she needed and the size and health of the live chicken she demanded he bring her.

On the third day, most of the men, as well as Sister Elspeth, were on the mend, keeping down the broth Sister Margriet made and not making as many runs into the bushes to relieve their other symptoms. Rurik believed they would be ready to travel soon.

But, it was the fourth day when fear struck deep in his heart, for he sought her out for his next task and found her lying unconscious by the stream where she went to wash out the linens and cloths she used to tend the sick. Without hesitating or even thinking it through, Rurik lifted her into his arms and rode the two hours back to the village. She was still unconscious when he carried her back into the inn and begged Thora to help him. When he finally placed her on the bed in the room up the stairs, he did not want to leave her side.

He tried to tell himself that he worried over the duty of bringing her to her father and that his honor was at stake in her survival of the journey, but his heart would not allow the lie.

Not to himself. Not any longer.

Rurik felt as though the gods of old were playing the worst kind of trick on him, as they'd played on generations before him, for in spite of everything wrong with the very notion of it, he knew he was falling in love with a nun.

Margriet tried to open her eyes, but the sheer exhaustion of these last days kept her from doing so. She felt scandalously lazy, for she knew the brief respite she'd planned had gone on much longer. The strange thing was, the surface beneath her felt like a bed instead of the mossy covering on the riverbank where she lay down. There were so many things yet to be done with the sick ones and she needed to let Rurik know where the rest of her herbs were…and where the clean linens were…and…

Soft voices and murmurings continued around her and, in spite of her intentions to wake, her body dragged her down into sleep once more. She felt the passage of time, but could not react to it. Then, she heard his voice saying her name and knew she needed to answer him.

"Rurik?" she whispered. Her throat was parched and words were difficult to form and force out.

A tiny splash of water on her lips soothed some of the dryness. Then, someone lifted her head and pressed a cup to her lips, urging her to sip. She did, drinking several mouthfuls slowly, until the cup was removed. Laying her head back, she savored the feel and the coolness of it as it moistened her tongue and throat.

"Many thanks," she whispered.

The watered ale must have revived her strength, for she was finally able to force her eyes to open and look around the darkened room. The shutters were closed and it sounded as if rain pelted them outside. A tallow candle sputtered on the table set next to the bed.

Bed? Shutters? Where was she? As she squinted in the dim light, she thought this looked like the chamber where she'd slept at the inn. But, she had fallen asleep on the bank of the river that rolled to the north and east of this village. How did she…?

"Ah, so yer awake now, Sister?"

"Thora?" Margriet tried to sit up, but her head spun making her so dizzy 'twas not worth the effort.

"Aye, Sister, yer back at my inn. *He* brought ye here yesterday, carrying on and on until ye were settled in."

"I did not carry on, woman," came the deep voice from the shadows of the room. "I was concerned about Sister when she fell ill."

Margriet turned her head and watched as he approached from the darkness, arms crossed over his chest, sword at his side, all brawn and, from his tone, lots of bite. Still, it was a relief to see him there.

"What happened? I only remember going to the river to launder the linens and closing my eyes for a moment."

Rurik walked toward her and reached out for a moment as though to take her hand. He threw a glance at Thora and then stood where he'd stopped.

"I found you unconscious there a short while later and could not rouse you. I…"

"Brought ye here, as I said," Thora finished, reaching over to tuck the blankets at her side. "Ye will be fine now, ye just needed yer rest."

Margriet felt as though a score of cattle had ridden over her bones. Aching in every place she could feel, she wondered if something else had happened to her.

"Fever?" she asked.

"Nay," both Rurik and Thora said at the same time.

"Puir wee lass," Thora said. She made clucking sounds then, shaking her head as she circled the bed, smoothing here and there, and staying just close enough to make Rurik back away to let her pass. "*He* had ye doing much too much more than ye should have. Tending all those sick men. Cooking and cleaning up their messes. Much too much."

The animosity between them was like something she could touch. Margriet looked from one to the other and back again, only to see identical expressions glaring at each other. 'Twould be comical if she did not hurt as much as she did. The groan was accidental, but it brought hostilities to a halt.

"Here now, Sister," Thora said as she brought the cup to her mouth again. "A wee small drink to help ye feel better."

"Thora, I would speak to Sister alone," he said in a growl.

"When she is feeling stronger," Thora began. "And when she is dressed suitably…"

Her words made Margriet reach up to check her wimple and veil and she found them both missing. Only a kerchief covered her hair.

"Now!" Rurik roared in a voice loud enough to make the roof rattle above them.

Thora was not a stupid woman, so she gathered her bowls and picked up her rags and scooted for the door. "I will be back," she whispered, not bothering to say it low enough so Rurik did not hear.

Margriet watched as Rurik closed the door and dropped the latch down to secure it. His expression softened as he turned to face her, filling with concern and even a measure of relief, if she read it correctly. He walked to the bedside, pulled over a bench and sat next to her.

"Another thing for me to beg your pardon for," he said softly. "I did not realize how hard you were working until it was too late."

"Rurik, please do not…" she began as she tried to sit up once more. This time, he slid his arm behind her to aid her and it made all the difference. And, with a pillow pushed behind her back, she could remain upright. The spinning inside her head slowed with each passing minute and that eased the stomach distress she felt growing. "I did what anyone would have done."

"But most would not have done so at the cost of their own health."

Uncomfortable with the personal nature of the topic, she changed it. "Is Sister Elspeth well?"

"She is and so are the rest of the men. All recovered due to your efforts," he said.

"And you and Sven? You did not become ill?"

"Nay. Thora said that others who ate the venison took ill, so you were correct in thinking that the cause. We were the only three who did not eat it that night."

So, she'd been right. No plague or contagion. Simply bad food.

"All recovered?" she asked again, just to be reassured. "No one lost to it?"

"Aye, Sister, all are well. Though as you mentioned, several did wish for death just before they improved." He smiled then and it tugged at her heart. "They will never admit this to you, but some also thought this was God's punishment for their sins."

This time, he winked ever so slightly, the merriment lightening his expression and making her smile as well. When she realized which sins they felt guilty of, Margriet looked away from his gaze.

"So, I have been here since yesterday?" She drummed her fingers on the covers.

"Aye. You have slept an entire day, a night and another entire day. 'Tis nigh to moonrise now." He stood and walked to one of the small windows, which he unlatched, allowing the shutters to open. "Though with the rain, 'tis most difficult to tell."

Margriet nodded, listening to the rain as it landed on the roof above and poured off, hitting the trees and ground below. The smell of it, fresh and clean, filled the room with each breeze. She breathed it in deeply, enjoying the calm that always followed for her.

"I ask your pardon, for slowing down your journey," she said.

"Since you are the reason we journey," he replied as he fastened the shutters closed again, "it seemed ill-advised to continue without you." Again, he tried levity.

"How long will we stay here?"

"As long as need be for you to feel strong enough to travel again."

"I will be ready on the morrow, Rurik."

He laughed then and the sound pierced her soul. His green eyes shone and his face looked lighter of many years and concerns. "Do not rush it, Sister. I will not put you in danger to save a day here or there in our journey."

Margriet smiled, feeling better not only because she was awake and sitting up, but also because he now talked to her and not at her. "Still…"

Her words were stopped when he reached out and took her hand in his. He closed his fingers around hers and raised them to his lips, pressing a gentle, almost reverent kiss on the top of her hand. She could not breathe in that moment. Sparkles of light danced before her eyes at the heated contact between them.

A forbidden contact.

Margriet tried to remember her feelings for Finn,

the man she knew she loved, the man who fathered her child, but when Rurik gazed at her in this way, she could not. Every word or promise she brought to mind rang false now as she stared at him. In a twist of luck, she spied the nun's habit on the nearby chair and it broke the spell between them.

"Nothing can happen between us, Rurik," she said, drawing her hand, however reluctantly, from his.

"Because of your vows?" he asked, leaning back away from her. "Do you think they will stand in defiance of your father's choice?"

"It matters not, I fear." Margriet shifted up in the bed to face him. "If these vows do not stand," Margriet said, referring to those she'd made with Finn and not anything to do with religious ones, "would my father choose you for me?" The expression gave her the answer before he could say any words. But she needed to know, since he likely knew more about her father and his bent in this than she did. "Would you be his choice?"

Rurik wanted to deny it and to admit that Gunnar would be proud to unite their families in a marriage between them, but such a match would be impossible. When Erengisl was counselor to Maolise and rose in power and married the old earl's daughter, he came as almost an equal in wealth and lands and power. Though absolutely faithful to Erengisl, Gunnar held no such place among the powerful families of Norway and Sweden.

And although it would be honor for Gunnar to join

his daughter to a son of Erengisl, his father had other plans and would forbid such a match. For his promise to Rurik for coming home and taking his place there was marriage to a woman of the royal house of Denmark. Gunnar's daughter was not high enough for Erengisl's son.

"No, I would not be his choice," he said quietly, allowing her to think all the wrong reasons for Gunnar's refusal. It mattered not why; it only mattered that the answer was no.

She seemed to need to push the point, for she asked it again. "So, if my vows dissolved on the morrow, there could be no match between us?"

He met her gaze then and made the declaration that would keep them apart, not only for the rest of this journey, but for the rest of their lives. "No match is possible between us, Margriet."

"So, it is clear then between us?"

It was a dismissal and Rurik wished with everything in him that giving her up and forgetting his desire and feelings for her were that simple. If he could only think *it is wrong so it does not exist,* he could walk away and worry not about her safety or her well-being or her future, married off in a bargain to a man she'd never met. But, for only the second time in his life, his heart did not believe it.

He stood then and walked to the window, opening it and listening to the storm outside. Why did this happen now and why in this manner?

His love for Nara had grown slowly, day by day,

from physical attraction to something deeper and less explosive. Oh, there was passion between them and lovemaking to fill their nights and many of their days, too.

But this—this was completely different. Was it only passion then? Lust and not love? He glanced over at her and knew she'd done nothing to entice him. If he liked her, it was because of what he saw in the woman beneath the habit.

She was kind to his men, not just when they were ill, but also as she spoke to them and taught them a new tongue. She was intelligent. From her use of strategy along the journey to her command of the situation when the sickness overtook them, she could organize and plan and implement as well as any man he'd known. She had backbone, for she'd stood up to him countless times during their short acquaintance and did not accept things simply because he said so.

And she had courage.

Courage enough to defend a convent against a party of warriors with only an aging shepherd and a few arrows as weapons.

Courage enough to admit the truth between them and confront it when he would rather ignore it.

He inhaled the smell of the storm and closed the shutters once more. Facing her, he nodded.

"Aye, 'tis clear between us, Sister," he said.

He saw the tear drop from the corner of one eye and run down her cheek, and wanted desperately to go to her. But, her courage demanded at least the same from him. So, without saying another word, he nodded and left the room.

The storm outside called to him and he ignored Sven's words as he passed him at the bottom of the stairs. Sister Elspeth would stay with Sister Margriet now that she was awake and, once the traveling party had regained their strength, they would leave for the north. Rurik strode to the door of the inn and opened it, walking out into the torrents of water and wind.

Mayhap he would be cleansed of his sins by the power of the storm? Mayhap the rains would wash away the desire that even now pulsed through him for her and sluice away the ache that built stronger with each breath he took for not having her in his life?

Rurik walked for as long as he could, as long as the winds howled and the rains poured down, hoping for an easement of his pain. When he found himself below her window as the clouds rumbled above him, he knew it would take more than that. He leaned against the side of the inn and slid down to sit there. And when dawn broke the next morning, he was still there.

Margriet struggled from the bed and staggered to the window just in time to see him walk away into the storm. The light that escaped from the inn's door shone on him until someone slammed it against the storm.

She should feel relief now that his attentions would stop, but she did not. She should be pleased that one less problem would follow her north and encumber any reconciliation she would have with her father and with Finn when she found him, but she was not. She should sense a clearer future now that the question of any involvement between them was answered, but she did not.

Instead, the rains outside covered the sounds of her sobs and the tears that poured down her cheeks. She stood, clutching the edge of the window, and watched him disappear into the downpour. 'Twas only Elspeth's assistance, when she arrived, that helped her manage the walk back to the bed.

After lying down, she tried to think on why this hurt so much. She certainly did not want him, for she'd learned that lesson only too well. Nor could she marry him, for she carried another man's bairn and her father would never permit it even if that were not the impediment. She certainly did not love him, for…there were so many reasons why she did not, could not, would not love him.

But lying there, as he left, she could think of none. And the pain in her heart told her that mayhap…

"Lady Margriet?" Elspeth said. Margriet wiped her eyes and looked at the girl. "Are you well?" She nodded. "And the bairn?" Another nod. "I was so worried for you when Sven told me how sick you were."

"Sven told you?"

"He is learning quickly," the girl said, a hint of a smile curving her mouth. "In truth, 'twas the other who said it and Sven repeated it."

"Rurik?"

"Aye." Elspeth nodded as she removed the head coverings and then lifted the tunic over her head. "Some of us were just waking when he found you. Lady, the way he screamed your name sent shivers down my spine." Elspeth shuddered again then. "Truly, I thought you must be dead."

"He was simply following my father's orders to keep me safe, Elspeth. Do not make more of it than that."

Elspeth's eyes grew wide and she shook her head as she unlaced her gown. "Nay, lady. He howled as though in pain himself, like a wolf that has lost their mate."

The girl looked at her and nodded now. "Leathen and Donald were surprised by it, for they said that Rurik goes from one woman to the next spreading his seed as a bee flits from flower to flower making…" Color crept into Elspeth's cheeks as she realized what she said. And to whom she said it.

"They spoke of such things to you?"

"Oh, nay, lady." She shook her head again and came to sit on the bed. "I overheard them when they did not know I was awake. They believe me a nun, and you, too, and would never speak of flitting to us."

"You must tell me if they are disrespectful, Elspeth. We must keep up our pretense." At the girl's frown, she added, "Keep up our disguise until we reach my father."

Margriet felt sleep's grasp grow stronger, even though she had slept for nearly two days straight. Thora's promised return with food was still to come, so mayhap talking would keep her awake. The thought of learning more about Rurik made her fight to remain so.

"Did you hear anything else about him? About Rurik?"

"Donald and Leathen told one of the others of how Rurik tried to tup his laird's wife when he first met her."

She gasped, shocked that he would be guilty of such a thing until she remembered his words to her.

I have lived the last thirteen years seeking pleasure where it may be, and have never met a woman I wanted who I could not have until you.

"And the laird did not kill him for such an insult?" Margriet still could not believe it true, for there must be more to the story. "I cannot believe my father would trust me in the care of a man who would…" She tried to say the words, but couldn't.

"Tup any woman who would spread her legs for him?"

Although Elspeth repeated the vulgar words obviously spoken by one of the men, she seemed to surprise even herself for she clapped her hands over her mouth as she finished saying them. "Forgive me, lady, I should not have repeated such things to you."

Margriet was completely and utterly confused now. Would she ever understand how men thought? Or why they did what they did? Just a short while ago, she would have been willing to gamble her father's fortune that Rurik had some deeper feelings for her. She would have sworn on God's Holy Bible that he was going to pledge that love to her before she stopped him. Now, she wondered if it was all nothing more than a way to batter her defenses down.

Elspeth must have known how her words bothered Margriet, for the girl grew quiet and prepared herself for sleep. Thoughts and fears and questions swirled inside her mind as she tried to do the same, but it was a long time before rest was granted to her that night.

And when it came, it was pierced with nightmares that terrified her and she awoke several times to her own choking screams. Elspeth shook her several times to wake her from terror's grip, and when morning did break, Margriet could swear she'd slept not a wink.

Thora's arrival brought a tray and the news that *he* said they were granted another day of rest. Apparently more storms were on the way and would hamper any good progress north. Margriet found her appetite restored and her strength rebounding after her collapse. When the sun forced its way through a break in the clouds late in the morning, she thought she might go for a short walk. After being reassured that Morag and Ragna had gone off to visit kin in another town for several days, she felt up to it. And so, with Elspeth in tow and Donald at their backs, they ventured out to explore the small village until the rains chased them inside again.

Chapter Twelve

"No church, Sister."

"Who cares for your immortal souls then?" she asked.

Margriet had thought to escape the inn, but Thora insisted on asking her all kinds of questions about the convent where they came from and her father's call home. Thinking to distract the woman long enough to get out, she moved toward the door.

"A priest usually travels through here about two times a year, spring and autumn, to bless the graves or baptize the newly born."

"And mass?" she asked, lifting the latch of the door and holding it open. "Surely, you hear mass more than that?"

Thora stopped at that, the blush in her cheeks revealing that she did not want to admit to such a thing. Harald called her from the kitchen and the woman excused herself to answer his call, leaving the nuns on their own.

Margriet made her escape as well, turning her face into the breezes that buffeted them along and promised more rain soon. For now, though, she and Elspeth, and Donald, walked down the worn paths of the village, and discovered that it was bigger than she first thought. They had traveled in from the south and headed out to the northeast, following the river's path. But, the village was not boxed in by the river and had expanded to the other bank. A small wooden bridge connected the two halves over the rushing water. They had just crossed the bridge when the shouting began.

Donald tried to guide them back to the inn, but Margriet wanted to see what was happening in the field next to the smithy's workshop. Following the noise and the growing crowd, she stopped and gasped at the sight before her eyes.

Sven and Magnus and Rurik, all stripped to the waist, fought each other at the same time. She'd never seen anything like it, she truly did not remember ever seeing men fight with swords, and she watched as they turned one on the other and then back against the third. The clashing of the metal against metal rang out loudly and made her wince with each blow delivered. And they did not limit themselves to only the blows of swords.

Elspeth grabbed her hand as they pushed each other aside and kicked from behind, always trying to gain control. The girl gasped so loudly when Sven tripped that he turned and saluted her with his sword as he regained his footing. Rurik used that momentary distraction to go on the offensive, slashing and thrusting with his sword until Sven had backed up across the whole field.

They laughed like loons as they alternated control of the match. And they called out insults to each other as they moved across the field, insults she tried not to hear. The villagers cheered them on, enjoying the display as much as those who were putting it on for them.

Margriet tried not to stare at Rurik's naked chest and the way the pale curling hair on it trailed down and disappeared below the belt of his breeches. He wore old-style gold armbands, carved with runes, that outlined the strong muscles of his upper arms. He glistened with sweat in spite of the cool air.

Magnus stumbled once and then again, and then was sent sprawling in the dirt by a blow to his back by Rurik. He climbed to his feet and bowed to the others, leaving the battle to them. When he faced the watchers, he saw them and walked to where they stood. Pushing his sweaty hair from his face, he laughed.

"If not for my recent illness, I could have won," he boasted to those listening.

"Of course, Magnus," she said, accepting his explanation as the truth. Margriet did not look away now, for Sven and Rurik moved so quickly that the end could come at any moment and she did not want to miss it. "Who has the advantage now?"

Magnus laughed again. "Rurik but plays as a cat

to a mouse now. He can end this whene'er he chooses. See now how he forces Sven to overextend himself." Magnus's comment made her watch more closely and she saw the truth in his words.

Now she noticed how the muscles of his legs tensed and relaxed as his stance changed, the power visible even at this distance. His breeches lay plastered against his legs, making it difficult not to see the strength and masculinity there.

Elspeth tugged on her sleeve and she realized the girl had not understood Magnus's words. When Margriet translated the words, Elspeth paled. Before she could explain any further, the crowd cried out as Rurik delivered two punishing blows to his opponent—the first knocked the sword from his hands and the next sent him to the ground on his back. Even she gasped now as Rurik placed the tip of his sword at Sven's neck.

"Stop!" the girl screamed shrilly, as she pulled away from Margriet and ran to the two men. "Stop!" she said again, in Norn, as she pushed against Rurik to force him and his sword away.

Margriet and those watching stood in surprise as Elspeth helped Sven to his feet after Rurik stepped aside. She and Magnus made their way across the field and watched with Rurik as Sven and Sister Elspeth walked back toward the inn.

Rurik shook his head and shrugged, while Margriet saw that the danger here had not been the battle at all. Did she try to explain Elspeth's behavior or not comment and hope it would fade from memory as the men talked excitedly about the battle and who delivered the best blows and who won? Deciding that discretion was her best weapon, she examined them and found both bleeding and covered in dirt.

"Come, it looks like you have wounds that need tending now," she directed as they both stared at her as though she'd lost her wits. "Look there," she said, pointing at Magnus's forearm. "That will need sewing to close it—" looking over at Rurik's chest and trying not to get lost in it, she nodded at his shoulder "—and there as well."

"Nun or not, is she not a bossy bit?" Magnus asked.

Margriet held her breath as he spoke the first words since their encounter the night before.

"Oh, aye. Thank the Almighty that you were sick those few days and missed the worst of it." Rurik winked at her then and she felt a light brighten her soul.

All would be well, she thought, as she followed the men back to the inn. They had each reconciled to the truth of their situation now and all would be well.

They left her to wash in the river and she slowed her pace to catch her breath—the breath that had left her at the sight of him, in tight breeches, moving as one with his weapon. At once, the consummate warrior and strong protector of legend.

The crowd pushed past her as she dawdled along and 'twas then she heard the voices of two of the men who traveled with him from Lairig Dubh.

"That's the old Rurik," Leathen boasted to those

from the north. "He favors two things in life and does them better than any man I know."

"And what would they be?" another called out.

"He loves to fight," Leathen offered as those around him laughed and pushed him about. "And he loves to f…"

The men shouted out, making it impossible to hear the final word, but Margriet needed no one to tell her. She knew without doubt the missing word.

She knew even more now that she'd felt the heat of his touch, the seductive invitation of his kiss and his formidable form and skills in battle. He was a man built to fight men and to f… Er, tup women.

And she prayed with equal measure that she would and would not ever discover it to be true.

The rest of the day passed more easily, now that the fight had both entertained and released some of the tension in the men. Rurik, especially, seemed at ease now, even though she had sewed two wounds to stop their bleeding. He argued that they were but flesh wounds and would heal, but she closed them with needle and thread, stopping short of demanding a bandage on them. Magnus sat quiet under her attentions as she patched his skin back together, as did Sven when they finally dragged him from the weeping Sister Elspeth's side.

Margriet tried to discourage such a thing with a sharp look and whispered warning, but the girl thought Rurik meant to kill Sven and now endangered their charade with her inappropriate concern for the man. She planned to speak to Elspeth after the evening meal.

The men carried out preparations all day, even as the rain started and stopped. Before dark fell completely, the supplies that would see them to the north coast were readied and packed and all was in good stead for an early morning departure.

Thora had tempted her and Elspeth from their room to eat in the common room with the others on the promise of no untoward occurrences, and Margriet was glad she'd done so. Some of the villagers gathered at the inn that night and Margriet could see that the men enjoyed the camaraderie after many days on the road.

She did notice that none of the men under Rurik's command overindulged in ale that night. Some, no doubt, were still feeling the aftereffects of the stomach ailment of a few days before. Others knew the morning would come quickly and that they needed a clear head and calm belly to ride out. It did not take long, once they'd eaten their fill and had a cup filled with ale in their hands, for talk to turn to the fight this morning. If she encouraged the direction of the talk, well, 'twas no matter.

"Tell me of Lairig Dubh and the clan that calls it home," she said while nodding to Leathen. His tongue seemed the loosest and a good place to start. And from his earlier comments, he knew much about Rurik.

"Connor MacLerie and his lady-wife make their

home there, Sister. It sits on a hill at the side of a river off in the west of Scotland. Connor is Earl of Douran and Laird of the MacLerie clan," he said, pausing to lift his cup in a salute. The other Scots joined him and nearly rattled the windows with their cry. "A MacLerie! A MacLerie!"

When she noticed that Rurik had joined them, she decided it was time to find out more, especially about the laird's wife and the supposed tupping. "Rurik, you lived there?"

"Aye, Sister, and I lived at other MacLerie holdings for my uncle is one of the elders of the clan and counselor to Connor."

He met her gaze, almost inviting more questions. She obliged.

"Your uncle is a MacLerie then?"

"My uncle is connected by marriage to the sister of the laird. I pledged to him and the laird when I could hold my sword straight and not embarrass myself—" he looked to the men who enjoyed some private joke at his words "—and better men I have yet to meet or serve." This time, only he offered the words. "A MacLerie!"

Now she could get to the heart of it. "And the laird's wife? From what clan did she come?"

His voice lowered to an almost reverent tone then and she could feel his true affection for the woman he spoke of now.

"Jocelyn came from the MacCallum clan, but has made Lairig Dubh her home and the Clan MacLerie her people. A good woman and a fitting mate for Connor," he finished and put his cup down. He leaned down and spoke words only meant for her ears as the chattering went on around them. "He was called the Beast of the Highlands before she came to him and she proved them all wrong about him and nearly at the cost of her own life."

"It sounds as though you care about her," Margriet offered, remembering the words spoken earlier about them.

"Aye, I do care. She is a good friend and a woman worthy to be married to the man I call Laird."

He emptied his cup and turned it over on the table so no more would be poured in it. He did not move from his seat on the bench, so Margriet thought him not ready to leave.

"And now you return to your father in Kirkvaw?"

She held her breath, waiting to find out if he would answer or not. He'd already said his mother was Scottish, so she wanted to discover more about his father.

"Aye, Sister. I return at my father's call, much like the prodigal son in your Good Book." He reached up and ran both hands over his head, wincing as he moved the area she'd sown.

"Does it still bleed?"

"Nay, it does but pull when I move it. As I said, 'tis but a flesh wound and not the worst I have ever suffered."

The men caught that bit and seized it, offering her

story after story of his courage and strength in battle. In each, he triumphed against great odds and she wondered how much was true and how much they embellished the story each time 'twas told. Margriet watched as he laughed at their words, never correcting and never adding to the stories, but nodding in recognition of some parts.

"Is battle like today's fight?" she asked him. She'd never seen a true battle, only read of them in books or heard stories told of them. Here was someone who had been in the fiery heat of them and lived to tell.

"Nay, Sister," he began. She noted that he called her that smoothly now, as though he finally believed it her calling. "Today was simply some exercise and training long overdue because of our journey." He turned and met the gaze of every one of their men before speaking again. "Training that will begin daily from here on. We will not arrive in the north as weaklings who have lost their ability to hold a sword. You teach them words and I will remind them of the sword."

His challenge was met with cheers. Obviously men cannot pass too many days without their weapons drawn and aimed at each other. Another thing about men she would simply not understand.

Rurik stood now and held out his hand to assist her to her feet. He also took a step to the side, successfully blocking Sven from approaching Elspeth to do the same. He did understand. They allowed, or forced, Elspeth ahead of them, so there was no possibility of her speaking directly to Sven. They entered the room and he stopped at the door. Not certain if he would come in or not, he then began to pull it closed. He stopped for a moment and widened it so that he could say something.

"Sister Elspeth," he whispered. "Sister Margriet would offer you some good counsel and I would urge you to think on her words."

Then, he did leave; the latch fell into place as the door closed tightly. Margriet turned to Elspeth, whose expression turned angry.

"Elspeth, you must understand…."

"That this is all a lie, lady? I do understand that," Elspeth interrupted. "Done for your benefit."

"And yours as well," she added. "I promised you a place in my father's house and a good match for a husband."

Elspeth tore the wimple and veil off and tossed it against the wall. Never had she seen the girl react like this—showing boldness where before had been only acquiescence. Now, she stood with hands on hips, and her chin thrusted out, looking like someone who would not accept what before had been acceptable.

"I have found a suitable man for husband."

Margriet gasped at her words. "Elspeth, you cannot think to marry him."

"He has spoken of his love for me."

Margriet did not know which pain felt worse within her—the one that said her young servant was going to be destroyed by the worthless words of a man promising love, or the one that spoke of her own destruction in the very same manner. Still, she could do something to prevent this young girl from the same downfall. She removed her own head coverings, taking several deep breaths to calm herself. She folded the items on the chair and began unbuttoning the tunic.

"Has he touched you?" she asked, comprehending the danger in that.

"He kissed my hand," Elspeth answered on a sigh.

"You are of common blood, Elspeth, and he, of noble. Think you his parents would allow a marriage between you?"

She said it plainly, for she knew that passion was already engaged between them. She did not wish to hurt the girl's feelings, but a servant girl, born and raised all her life in a small secluded convent, was more suitable a bride to the local farmer than to this nobleman's son who walked at the highest levels of court.

"We must continue this masquerade until we reach my father's house. Then, if you still want him and he will have you after finding out the truth, it can be sorted out then."

"But, lady…" Elspeth began.

"I will hear no more of this," Margriet said calmly and sternly. "You know the reason I must wear this nun's habit, for protection against them—" she nodded at the door where the sounds of the men still carousing could be heard "—but also to protect this from disclosure." She placed her hand on her rounding belly. "I, too, was promised love, Elspeth. You would be wise to see if a man's promises in the heat of passion are kept to me, before losing all you have to give to someone else."

Tears streamed down the girl's face as she stared at Margriet's belly and the proof of her sin. Margriet's throat tightened as she waited for Elspeth to accept or reject her words and their agreement of reward at the end. The only acknowledgment she received was a curt nod, before the girl turned away to prepare for bed.

Thora had provided a jug of water and a basin, so they each took a turn, washing their face and hands. Margriet longed for a steamy, hot bath that she could soak in for hours and it was the first thing she would ask for at her father's house. For now, the small comfort was a welcomed thing. The air was heavy between them now—not a word was spoken through the rest of the time it took to ready for sleep. As she lifted the blankets to climb in, Elspeth approached with a cup.

"Lady, I forgot that Thora left this for you. She said it will help you regain your strength for the journey ahead."

"But you were the one who became ill, Elspeth, you should have it."

The girl shook her head and held it out to her. When Margriet would have argued, Elspeth whispered, "Probably best for the bairn as well."

She sniffed at the cup and was surprised by its pleasant aroma—not like the medicinal potions brewed at the convent. This smelled of cloves and honey and something else she could not name. Margriet sipped a small taste and it washed smoothly over her tongue and down her throat. So smoothly, that she took another and another until she'd finished it.

She would ask Thora for her recipe and for what uses this brew worked, for it was tasty and easy to drink, two that couldn't be said of curative brews. Margriet thanked Elspeth for it and climbed into the bed, planning to enjoy her last night on its soft surface. They would spend about five more days riding north before reaching any village or town that offered such comforts. Five or six nights of sleeping on the hard—and growing cold—ground. She shivered as she thought of it.

Soon, the men downstairs grew quiet and a deep warmth seeped into Margriet, pulling her, pushing her toward sleep much faster than was her custom. With so many concerns and worries, sleep usually came upon her slowly. This night, she felt it dragging her down into its dark fog.

Chapter Thirteen

The Earl's Hall
Kirkvaw

The interruption came at a very bad time for Thorfinn, but Sigurd's timing was never good. The success of his work, however, was indisputable and so the man stayed alive and in his employ. Not wanting to delay the news from Caithness, he called out permission to enter. If Sigurd was surprised by the sight before him, he did not reveal it.

Good man.

Smart man.

The whore knelt between his legs, her naked body blocking the sight of her mouth on his cock, but Sigurd did not need to see the particulars to understand the situation. When she tried to lift away from him, apparently believing that Sigurd's presence meant an end to hers, he lifted the cane and let it land on her bare back. A hand in her hair told her that the bite of her teeth at this moment of pain would simply bring more of it. The bitch was in heat and, wisely, dove down, taking him in deeper as she knew he liked.

His minion bowed and waited for permission to continue. Thorfinn did not grant it just yet, as he let the whore work on his cockstand for now, wanting it to be hard and large and near to exploding in her mouth when he heard good news about his enemies' journey. She added some noises that made it sound as though she was enjoying her work, but he knew it was only for show. Again, he struck her with the cane, this time on her bottom where the marks of his previous attention bloomed red and bloodied. Pain and pleasure were such a heady and intoxicating mix when delivered just right.

He knew it stung—he'd made sure of it when he aimed for just a certain spot on the torn skin of her arse—and he knew that she wanted to cry out. Now Thorfinn waited, almost hoping that she would.

Delivering pain excited him and her newness under his hand was more thrilling to him than using someone broken in to his varied tastes. He caught Sigurd's gaze at that moment as he, too, waited to see her response. When her mouth moved down and up on him again, Thorfinn was partly disappointed, but the pleasure of her tight mouth and throat made up for it.

Now, on to business.

"Well, Sigurd. You have news for me? If you

finish quickly and it is good news, mayhap you could join me?"

He stroked the cane down the whore's back, sliding the piece of wood between the mounds of her arse, offering a reminder of something they'd done before when sharing a woman.

Sigurd's face went blank for a moment, a sign of his unwillingness to share in his lord's largesse. Well, this one would be used up soon enough without his help. Thorfinn petted her head as she continued, much as he would pet an animal. Sigurd gave his report.

"My lord, they will be delayed by four more days due to illness."

Thorfinn laughed then, enjoying the news and the pressure that built in his testicles. "Anyone die of it?"

"Nay, my lord. I did not think you wanted anyone killed." Sigurd paused now and gestured to the woman. "I would prefer to deliver this in private, my lord."

"Unless you want to suck my cock in her place, that is not your choice to make, Sigurd." Thorfinn leaned down and whispered loudly to the slut. "And if she wants her skillful little tongue to not be cut out at its root, she will use it only as I order and say nothing to no one."

The whore was a quick learner, for there was almost no hesitation in her efforts now as he delivered that warning. With his free hand, he motioned for Sigurd to go on. "What was the cause of this sickness?"

"Tainted meat, my lord."

Thorfinn laughed out loud now at his man's re-sourcefulness. "Your idea, Sigurd? I commend you on it."

"Not mine to take credit for, my lord, but I will pass on your praise to the one who did." When Sigurd would have spoken again, he held up his hand.

The whore's tricks were working and his sac and rod tightened as his release approached. He took in a slow breath, trying to draw it out, but he felt his seed begin to flow. Pulling her by the hair off his cock, he watched as the pearly liquid sprayed over her face and neck. A few moments and he emptied all that had built up within him.

Tossing her aside, he ordered, "Wash your mouth and your arse, I want it clean for the next time." When she backed away and reached for her garments that lay next to his chair, he used the cane on her out-stretched hand. "I said nothing about covering your-self, bitch." Without raising her head or eyes to him, she crawled back and away, toward the corner where a basin sat waiting.

Thorfinn tugged his breeches and tunic back into place and stood, accepting the cup that Sigurd knew he would want. Drinking deeply from it, he waited for the rest of the news.

"So, four days more that my father will fret over," he said. "How wonderful! Anything else, Sigurd?" He emptied the wine in one more mouthful, anxious to return to more pleasurable pursuits.

"It may be more than that, my lord. There seems to be some kind of distraction growing that may stop them for a bit."

"A distraction, Sigurd? That sounds interesting. What kind of distraction?"

Sigurd glanced over at the corner of the chamber, where the slut washed herself in the shadows. "One of the feminine kind, my lord."

Thorfinn smiled. Women held such promise, for sexual pleasure, as weapons and pawns, even as whores and slaves. Gunnar's daughter had provided him several evenings of pleasure, though of the dullest sort, but would, if his plans succeeded, be an outlet for his more creative efforts soon.

"Make it so, Sigurd. Any delay is a good one." Thorfinn put the cup on the table as he walked with Sigurd to the chamber's door. His man was holding something back from him, waiting until the last to reveal it. He could tell by the nervous way Sigurd's eyes kept darting to the door. "Something else?"

"She is a nun."

Of all the things he expected to hear, that was not one of them. And it was truly a shock. "A nun? Gunnar said nothing about her taking vows."

Thorfinn thought back to his encounters with her those months ago and did not remember that particular detail ever being mentioned. Well, would someone sneaking out to seek pleasure from a stranger even reveal such a thing? Not that it would have stopped him from taking her maidenhead, for—nun or not—she had all the bodily openings and crevices any woman should have to see to his needs.

Any differences from one slut to the next were inconsequential as long as they did not interfere in his plans or his pleasure. Now though, the thought of her being a nun when he ruined her aroused him. Damn, he wished he'd known at the time!

"Gunnar does not know," Sigurd added.

Thorfinn chortled at this news. Could it get any better? His day brightened and his ire at being interrupted disappeared now in light of this. One more humiliation for Gunnar. Sigurd had earned a reward for this parcel of information.

"You are dismissed, with my praise for work well done. Unless you have changed your mind and wish to stay? I have not broken her yet in either place. You can have your choice and I'll watch," he offered, in such good spirits that he felt a generosity that was not usual for him. He gestured to the woman who walked toward them, head bowed, blood and seed cleaned from her naked body, and ready to begin anew.

"I have much to do, my lord," Sigurd offered as he pulled the door opened and left. The man was too dour for his own good.

Pushing the door closed, Thorfinn turned to find the whore kneeling at his feet. If she thought his change in mood, now much lighter for the news Sigurd brought, would mitigate his attentions toward her, she was wrong. Thorfinn left her and walked to the wooden cabinet that held his assortment of implements of discipline.

Lifting one of the whips, his favorite for the exquisite torment it gave when lashed with it, he let it unroll and drag at his side, the metal tips on each strand scraping along the floor as he walked back to her. She stared at it and then at him as he cracked it over her head and then on the floor where she knelt. The third time it bit her on the shoulder. Real fear entered her eyes then and she shook her head when she met his gaze.

Ah, he thought, his cock hardening once more, there was always much to be done and so many ways to enjoy it.

Chapter Fourteen

"Margriet? You must wake up."

She heard it, had heard it the several others times it tried to pierce the darkness that held her, but again, she could not answer.

"Margriet!" he called louder, making her head throb. Or did her head already throb and his voice made it worse.

Finally when she could fight it no more, she opened her eyes to find four faces staring down at her—Rurik, Thora, Harald and Donald. Donald? She looked around to find the missing person who should be there—Elspeth.

"Elspeth?" She pushed up on her elbows and searched for some sign of the girl.

The silence that greeted her told Margriet that something was wrong. Rurik ordered the others from the room and waited for Donald to escort Harald and his wife to the main floor. Then he turned back to her.

"Why did you ask for Elspeth?"

Margriet slid back, drawing the blankets to her neck as she moved and righting the kerchief now in place on her head. Thora, it seemed, always watched out for her modesty.

"She was very upset last evening, Rurik." She noticed the light streaming in and knew it was morning. "What hour is it?"

"Almost noon."

"Nay, it cannot be," she said, shaking her head. "You said we were to leave just after dawn." He sat on the edge of the bed now and she shifted to give him room.

"Elspeth has disappeared."

It could not be so. They'd slept in the same bed. She would have known because she was the one who did not fall deeply asleep; she was the one who woke at any noise.

Unless something had caused her to do otherwise? Margriet looked around the room and saw the cup on the small table next to the bed.

"When did you see her last, Sister?"

"Last night. After you left, I spoke to her about Sven and... Did you ask Sven about her?"

The stern expression warned her of his answer before he spoke the words. "He is missing as well."

"Rurik! We must find them," she cried out. Grabbing the end of the blankets, she needed to get out of bed and dress so they could search. "I beg you to move so I can rise."

He did not heed her, but stayed where he was.

"Did you hear anything? Anyone else in the room? Anything amiss."

Margriet sat back and thought about Elspeth's behavior. "She was crying when I finished speaking to her, but then she offered me a draught that Thora sent up. To make me stronger."

"A sleeping draught, I fear, so that you would miss her departure," he offered. "I suspect that Thora knows not of it."

He stood then, and pointed to the gown thrown over the chair. "Dress and come down and we can decide what to do next."

She did not know which surprised her more—that he did not question her involvement or that he was about to include her in his decisions about how to proceed. "We?"

"I learned at our first encounter that it is better to work with you than against. And, truth be told, you demonstrated that you can think clearly when everyone was taken ill. I could not have managed all of them without your knowledge and hard work."

Speechless for the first time in so long, Margriet fell back against the headboard and just looked at him. The good sisters complimented her occasionally, but the thrill of this one, that he thought highly of her abilities, warmed her heart. 'Twas only sad that it came at such a time as this.

"Now, dress and come down. I will have Thora prepare you something to eat and drink and I will watch her do it to be certain it contains nothing else." He stood and left without looking at her.

"Rurik," she called before the door could close completely.

He stopped and waited for her to speak, half in and half out of the room.

"Will he...will he...she is..." She could not say the words she was thinking, but he understood her mumbled words.

"He is a man of honor who would never take advantage of a holy innocent."

He used that tone that men did when they were completely convinced of a thing. Such as honor. The tone that warned her from arguing—nay, from even thinking for a moment—that he was not correct about his friend and his honor. Rurik's faith in his friend was only undermined by one small thing that was unknown to him when he made that declaration.

Elspeth was not a holy innocent and neither was she. Although Elspeth certainly was an innocent, she was neither. And being the sinner she knew herself to be, Margriet could not admit this all to Rurik. So, she reasoned, Elspeth was safe with Sven so long as Sven believed her to be a nun. Margriet could not think beyond that now.

He looked at her as though waiting for any other concern to be voiced and then, with a nod, strode from the room and pulled the door closed behind him. With nothing else to say, Margriet lost no time in following his instructions and within minutes entered the common room where Rurik waited. She walked in to hear Harald and Thora's denials of their involvement in either the drugging of Sister Margriet or helping Sven and Sister Elspeth to leave unnoticed.

"I will burn this place to the ground if I find you are lying to me, Harald." Margriet was tempted to ask if that was his method of dealing with problems, but held her tongue. He turned as she approached. "Thora swears she sent no draught to you last evening, Sister."

"It seems that Elspeth had her mind set on this."

"I canna believe that she would run off wi' him," Thora sobbed into a piece of linen. "A nun, no less! A holy sister! An innocent led into debauchery…"

'Twas then that Rurik stopped her with a look. Harald assured him once more that they knew nothing and dragged his wife back toward the kitchen. When they had gone, he moved a bench out so she could sit. Only he, Leathen and Donald remained with her.

"The men?"

"I sent two out in each direction leading away from the village to see if they could find evidence of their path." He paused and stared at their small group. "I wanted to keep this discussion to only this number," he said. "'Tis a matter best handled with discretion."

"Why would Sven take her away, Rurik?"

"Why would she leave with him, Sister?"

She was torn between telling him the truth and keeping it to herself. There was a part she could share.

"She believed he loved her."

Rurik's gaze faltered for a moment, but the other two were frank in their disbelief.

"He would never dishonor her in that way, Sister," Donald argued. "Never."

"I have known him since the time we were we'ans, Sister. He has respect for the church and all that belongs to it," Rurik added.

Leathen shook his head so hard, Margriet thought it would loosen from his neck.

"And if she was not a nun? Would he hold her in respect then?"

The only sound in the room was the fire crackling in the hearth. She was convinced they'd even stopped breathing at her disclosure. In truth, she could not believe she'd said it aloud.

"Not a nun?" Leathen repeated the words as though she'd said them in Greek instead of Gaelic.

"Get out," Rurik ordered. "Say nothing about this to any of the others, especially not those from Orkney."

Donald and Leathen were quick on their feet when they wanted to be and her words coupled with Rurik's order gave them cause to move. The silence was harsher still when it was only the two of them.

"I am waiting to hear your explanation, Sister? How is Sister Elspeth not a nun?"

He leaned back and watched her with such a dangerous air that she feared revealing even part of the truth. With one ankle resting on the other knee, he sat waiting. She would rather deal with an angry Rurik, such as the one who stood outside the convent gates, than this quietly deadly one.

She opened her mouth to speak, but nothing came out the first time. Or the second. It struck her that fear was a powerful silencer. As though he was being kind, Rurik reached out, poured some ale into a cup and handed it to her.

"Pardon my inhospitality, Sister. I forgot you have not broken your fast yet this morn. Should I call Thora for some bread and cheese?"

She drank some ale down in one gulp, but there would be no way to make food get down her throat now. Not with the way he glared at her across the table. Not with the way danger rolled off of him in waves, like the musk of a predator. Not when he repeatedly clenched and relaxed both his jaws and his fists.

"Nay," she cried out. "I need no food. Only ale."

He lifted the metal pitcher as though it were empty and filled her cup once more. "Enough?" he asked in a quiet voice that set her nerves on edge.

Margriet sipped from the cup and nodded, trying to formulate an answer to his question.

"Now, explain to me how she is not a nun?"

His foot bobbed now, rising and dropping in time with some internal measure. His jaw still twitched, but he had opened his hands and placed them on the table in front of her. It made her more nervous.

"We feared for her safety," she said.

"We?"

"Mother Ingrid and I. When you and your men

showed up at the convent making demands and yelling and scaring everyone with your…"

She would have continued, but now his eyebrow began to carry on the same twitching movement that hers did when she was tense. Knowing what it meant forced her to stop making excuses.

"When Elspeth offered to travel with me, Mother and I thought the habit would protect her against 'the ravenous hungers that men experience,' as Mother described it."

She would swear he fought a smile just then, but no one would describe the expression on his face as a smile.

"So, instead of relying on my honor and that of my men's as I swore it to you, and on your father's wisdom in making the choice of who would escort you home, you decided a piece of clothing would protect the girl?"

"Not just a piece of clothing, Rurik, a nun's habit. Men behave differently around one."

In that moment, too many thoughts were crossing to and fro in his mind to make any sense of her thinking in this. Truly, at that moment, he wondered how he ever thought her clear-minded. Instead of telling him the truth, that Elspeth was her companion, she'd lied in some ill-gotten plan to protect her virtue. It was incomprehensible.

No, it was just like a woman.

"Let us begin anew, here, Sister Margriet. Who is Elspeth?" He clenched his teeth together to keep from swearing and cursing the way he wanted to. Rurik feared that if he began, he would not stop, and they still needed to find Sven and the girl.

"Elspeth is the daughter of one of the landowners near the convent."

"A commoner?"

"Aye."

"Betrothed?"

"Nay."

"Taken vows of any kind in the convent?"

"Nay."

"Intending to stay with you in Orkney?"

"Well, I do not intend to stay in the Orkneys, Rurik. I am only returning long enough to convince my father to give me leave to…"

He knew her concise answers could not continue forever, but he held his hand up to stop her. "Did she intend to stay with you in the Orkneys?"

She sighed then and nodded her head. "I promised her a place in my father's household if she wanted it and a chance to make a good match."

He stood then, unable to sit any longer. If he had known this, he could have prevented trouble. "Did she say anything about Sven to you? Last night?"

A blush crept up her cheeks, making it obvious that the girl had told her something. Something she thought able to manage on her own. Instead she'd ended up drugged and sleeping while the two crept away at some time in the night.

"She claimed he loved her."

"Did he say that?"

"Does any man?"

He slammed his fist down at that comment, loud enough to draw Thora from the kitchen. Sister Margriet waved her away before he could yell or threaten and they were alone yet again.

"What did you tell her last night…when she told you he loved her?"

"She said Sven loved her, not that he had declared it in any way."

Was it possible for a man's head to explode atop his shoulders? Rurik felt as though his would at any moment. "And you said what?"

"Rurik, we both saw them after the fight. We both know that she is not of the same standing as he, that her place would be as a servant in his house or a leman in his bed. That nun's habit was the only thing standing between Sven and her…virtue."

'Twas the truth, as much as he'd like to argue against it. Still, if Sven thought her a nun, he would not dishonor her. If he thought her of the lower class, then…

"You see, do you not?" Margriet asked with a smugness in her voice that spoke of being right.

"But did he think her a nun when they left?" he fired back.

Her silence was not nearly as satisfying as he'd hoped. And when he noticed the tears gathering, he felt like the worst of villains.

"'Tis all my fault," she whispered. "I told her it

would work. I told her she would be safe until we reached my father's house. That she could tell him the truth and learn how it stood between them. Now…now…"

Her blubbering could not have shocked him more if she'd stood naked while doing it. Nay, that was the wrong image to take to mind while blaming another man for doing exactly what he'd done.

Coveting a nun.

Falling in love with a woman denied to him for many reasons.

When the tears began to fall, he did what he'd seen Connor do many times to soothe Jocelyn—he moved closer, put his arm around her shoulders and pulled her close. God Almighty, it felt good to hold her close and comfort her. A few minutes passed and she quieted against him. Reluctant to let the moment go and yet knowing he must, he leaned away and waited for her to regain control.

"Do you have any idea of where they might have gone?" he asked quietly. "Does she have family anywhere?"

Sister Margriet dabbed her eyes as she shook her head. "None that I ken." She sniffled then. "Would he offer her marriage? Would his family allow it?"

"He might wish to, but unless there was something of benefit, they would not permit him to marry so far beneath them."

As far beneath him as Margriet was beneath his own standing. In Sven's situation, wealth or connections could make the difference, but the girl had neither.

"Should we not follow them? Mayhap if we reach them in time…" She paused and her bleak eyes said she did comprehend the truth of it, no matter what her soft heart wanted to believe.

"I cannot follow them unless you are safe, and this would seem to be the safest place for you to wait." He looked around at the worn-down building. "Well, once we have word of their direction, and I suspect they travel on ahead of us, we can get on the road, too." He stood now and looked out the small window to the place where his men gathered. Rurik would need to tell them something.

"I would go speak to the men, give them some story about what has happened."

"Do they know? Did Sven confess anything to Magnus or one of the others?" She stood now, and smoothed her hands down the coarse tunic.

"I spoke to Magnus, who was shocked by this. He saw…they all saw her display yesterday, but thought she was overwrought from being ill and from Sven's kindness to her then. None expected this."

He opened the door and followed her into the yard next to the inn. The horses were gathered, packed with supplies and ready to ride. A pile of discarded sacks lay nearby, from the horses whose riders now needed speed to catch the couple. As he calculated, those horses would need to rest before they could travel north, so they would lose another day. One day, if Sven took her toward the islands, more if he rode in any other direction.

She waited by the door of the inn, while he spoke to the two groups, Scots and Northerners, offering no explanation but that the couple was gone without word and ordering that no assumptions be made until they were found. A word to Donald and Leathen separately assured that they would not share the revelation they'd heard about Elspeth with any of the others.

Rurik felt guilty in not sharing the information with Magnus, but something held him back. He wondered if Sven's disappearance was part of something else, for something had dogged their path since the first letter from his father. Each time arrangements were made, they needed to be changed for some reason or another. Then, when they were making good time, the illness hit. Now this. An uneasy feeling tickled his thoughts, but he could not see the whole scheme yet.

The day passed slowly and when the noon meal was offered, no one felt like eating. Later in the day, he allowed Donald and Leathen to take Sister Margriet to walk along the river, with a special warning about her clumsiness where water was concerned. The glare he got for that made him smile. If she was angry at him, mayhap she would not worry so much about the girl.

'Twas nigh on sunset when three of the four searching groups returned as ordered after finding no sign of the couple. As he suspected, Sven was heading home. The arrival of one of the final two men sent out this morn only confirmed it. The problem was that they were now separated by a day in time and distance and that would grow to be more with each passing day.

For it was easier for two people to travel faster than the group under his command. He hoped that the man tracking them could stay close enough and keep watch until they met up again, most likely in Thurso. As he was checking the inn for the final time and taking his place at the bottom of the stairs, Rurik was struck by the feeling that he was being led into a trap.

By whom or for what reason, he knew not. But years of fighting and watching his back taught him not to ignore such things. His life and the lives of those he guarded had been protected when he listened to the warnings from within. He would not begin to ignore them now.

The next week moved forward at an agonizing pace, for the weather turned bad and hampered their journey every day. Because the winds and rain came every day, they could only ride several hours instead of most of the day. Margriet still instructed the men in Norn and Gaelic as they rode, but her joy in it seemed diminished now. Margriet seemed a different person, still blaming herself for Elspeth's disappearance.

The next problem was her health and, although the stomach ailment of the first days did not return, she was exhausted by midday and could not stay upright on her mount. Because there was no other way to continue on, or so he told himself, he began carrying her on his horse, first riding pillion and then, after she nearly fell off when sleep overtook her, held in front of him. She argued the first time she woke in his arms, wrapped and kept dry and warm in the length of tartan wool he'd brought from the MacLeries, but soon even she seemed to accept it.

When they passed the final village and he knew they grew close to Thurso, he sent men on ahead to meet with an old friend of her father's who'd promised them food and shelter. The man's estate was south of the town, which suited Rurik, for he could leave half of his men there to see to Margriet's safety and comfort and send the other half to Thurso to find Sven and Elspeth.

The unusual arrangement he'd made with the man was to have use of the house without any others present. When they arrived, Rurik found it all as he'd asked—a well-stocked larder, fresh horses for their use and clean beds. There was even a barn large enough to house most of the men.

Within two days, Magnus had secured places on a ship going north to the islands and discovered Sven's hiding place. Now, he waited only for nightfall to uncover the truth.

Chapter Fifteen

Margriet had finished her prayers and lay completely awake in the large bed. This was the one comfort she could become accustomed to—a soft feather bed on top of ropes that kept her off the hard ground while she slept. This was nothing like the pallet on which she slept at the convent, nor the bed at the inn that she'd shared with Elspeth. This one was piled high with pillows and blankets and even some animal skins to keep her warm.

And they did.

The weather was changing and the cooler air crept in as autumn approached. She dreaded going north now, in a boat that would be tossed about on the sea. Margriet wondered though, as she had walked around the perimeter of the house before she retired, whether it was the boat or the destination she feared the most.

Now, when sleep should be coming, it did not. Although Rurik tried to hide it from her, she knew that he'd found Sven and Elspeth, and was going to confront them this night. She could not imagine the outcome, for no matter which way she turned it over in her mind, she could see no good end.

If Sven knew Elspeth's truth, and she prayed Elspeth had revealed no other secrets but her own, she doubted the girl was still a virgin. Rurik could not demand marriage between them, as they were not equal for the girl's honor to matter in that way.

All she could do was wait and pray, both for the well-being of all involved and for forgiveness for her part in this. If she had not resisted her father's call home—nay, if she had no reason to fear her father's call—none of this would have happened to Elspeth. The girl would be safely living at the convent until her parents made arrangements for her marriage to a suitable man they knew. Now, and only because Margriet had dragged her into this charade, the girl would suffer.

She drifted in and out of sleep, awaiting some word from Rurik on his return. The moon rose high in the clear sky that night and its beams of light lit the chamber where she slept through several windows high on the walls. Then, a noise brought her awake and she found him standing over her. Brushing the hair out of her face, she tugged the blankets up to cover her.

"Did you find them? Is Elspeth well?" she asked.

Instead of answering her queries, he turned and walked out. Confused, Margriet climbed from the bed, found a robe and pulled it on as she followed him. The house was not large but it felt as if she ran for miles to catch up with him, reaching him in the larder where he poured ale from a skin.

"Rurik? Tell me what happened, I beg you."

'Twas the wrong thing to say, for he turned on her, forcing her against a wall with his form and his height. He stopped then and took a step back and away from her. She caught sight of her wimple and veil, now crushed in his fist. Margriet was about to try to tuck her hair in the back of the robe when he laughed. A horrible sound, it was filled with pain and anger and none of the amusement a laugh should carry.

He drank the cup empty then filled it again. When that was done, he filled it yet again. Drinking it in two swallows, he threw the empty cup to the floor and wiped his mouth on the sleeve of his shirt.

"Do you know that I was actually jealous of Sven for following his heart? I thought him courageous for claiming the woman he loved, regardless of their situation or the outcome."

Margriet shook her head at such an admission. They had fought the attraction between them and overcome it, had they not? They understood their place, even when their hearts tried to say otherwise. And now he would applaud Sven for forgetting all that?

"You found them?"

"Aye, found them and confronted them tonight in town. They are married, damn the consequences."

Margriet inched along the wall until she reached

the doorway leading back into the kitchen. He was unpredictable tonight, hurt in some way that she could not determine and filled with anger. His next words made it all too clear.

"What did I do that made you believe lying to me was better than the truth?"

The pain in his gaze nearly brought her to her knees. "I did not mean…"

"Did you think me too far beneath you to offer the truth? Did you not believe your father would choose someone worthy enough to be your escort? Is a bastard not good enough for the truth?" He held out the head covering to her, but drew it back as she reached for it. Tearing it in pieces, he threw the strips of linen and cloth on the floor. "Elspeth told me the truth— you also hide behind the clothing of a nun."

"You must understand, Rurik," she tried to explain. "I was in fear of my…"

Even she could not speak the lie and say she thought him a threat to her life. He'd proven over and over during their journey that her safety was the most important thing to him. By his every word and action, she knew to the depths of her soul that he cared deeply for her.

"I swore to protect you, Margriet, and instead you mocked me at every step. Did you and Elspeth laugh when I apologized for kissing you that night by the river? Or when I thought you had died and felt the very soul within me being ripped asunder?"

Margriet saw no way out of this. Like a wounded

animal, he growled out his pain and nothing she said would make a difference now. The worst of it was that he was right—she should have trusted him, at least about not taking vows in the convent. But by the time she realized that she could trust him, she was beginning not to trust herself and the dangerous attraction between them was growing.

She edged her way toward the kitchen, hoping one of the men would come in and interrupt this before he did something he would regret. Strangely, she still felt no fear of him, even as he grabbed her hand and pulled her into his arms.

"Or when I admitted my love to you even though we knew the impossibility of such a thing existing between us?"

He brought his lips down on hers and plundered her mouth with an intensity and power she had not thought possible. With one arm around her waist and the other hand in her loosened hair, he kissed her over and over, taking all from her and demanding even more. Her body felt not her own as he gripped the top of the robe and pulled it off her, leaving only the thin chemise between them.

"Is that what you feared from me?" he whispered harshly.

If Finn's kisses and caresses were love, then this must be complete possession, for she felt as though they breathed as one and not two. His hand slipped between them now and cupped her breast, setting her on fire and making every secret place throb in want of more. Her mind screamed out for her to stop, to stop him, but her heart ached for this. To be wanted with such abandon, with such passion, with such love, was something she could not deny.

He eased her down on top of the robe and separated only long enough to tug his shirt off over his head. Then he was covering her, heating her coldness and enveloping her in his desire. His mouth captured hers again and he plunged his tongue deeply inside, touching hers and dancing with it, suckling on it and giving his for her exploration.

"Or did you fear this?"

"Rurik," she moaned. "We cannot…"

Any protest was lost then as he caressed her breasts and moved down to kiss them. The cloth of the chemise was no barrier to sensation, for she could feel the stubble on his chin and the edges of his teeth as he grazed the sensitive nipples. Her hands fell away as he suckled on them, first through the chemise and directly on her burning skin when he ripped it apart.

"I did not want to pursue you because I thought you were a nun, Margriet, but I stopped," he said, as he reached down and tugged the edge of the shift up over her legs, "because you told me to." With one of her legs trapped now under his, she held her breath as he slid his hand ever closer to the tender spot between her legs.

Panting, she fought for control now, losing that battle with each inch his strong hand advanced. She grabbed for his wrist, but it did no good. He covered her mouth with his once more as he dipped his fingers into the wet cleft at the juncture of her thighs and she moaned at the exquisite pleasure of finally feeling his touch in that most intimate of places.

"Without that lie between us any longer—" he kissed her again and stroked her deep and hard as he taunted her "—as only a woman to a man," he whispered as her pleasure built, "will you stop me now?"

She prayed now, for her traitorous body would not stop. Even the hand she placed on his wrist pushed him on, guiding him and urging him faster and deeper. His hardness thrust against her hip as he continued to touch her, inflaming her body until she was ready to beg for release. When he reached down and freed his manhood, rubbing himself now against her bare skin, her legs fell open to accept him. He lay on top of her and just as he shifted to enter her, he asked her one final time.

"Do you stop me, Margriet?"

She thought herself lost to the passion and the pleasure, but with his weight fully on her, Margriet felt a strange sensation that reminded her of the other secret she held, the one carried within her. Now, like a cold wind, the truth thrust forward and she grabbed his shoulders, looking into his eyes and making him see her.

"I cannot do this, Rurik. 'Tis wrong."

He stopped and shook his head at her words. "I will not dishonor you, Margriet. I offer you all that I have to give."

She pushed at him now and he rolled off her, lying by her side, breathing heavily as she considered the only thing she could do now. She may have lied to him on this journey, but she could not deceive him any longer.

"I cannot accept, Rurik, for there is another secret I hide," she said, taking his hand and sliding it over her belly, over the fullness there that could not be missed or mistaken. The layers of heavy cloth in the nun's habit had done their job covering it, but now, lying naked with nothing between them, there could be no misunderstanding.

She knew the moment he realized what he was feeling. He pulled his hand back and stared at her as though she was a stranger, and in some ways, she must be. He sat up and backed away from her, as she admitted what she had feared him discovering from their first meeting.

"It matters not that you love me or I love you, Rurik, for I have given my honor away."

The house was empty at his orders, for he wanted no one to overhear the conversation he planned with "Sister" Margriet. When he'd confronted Sven and his new wife Elspeth, his surprise gave way to profound shock as she revealed that Margriet was not a nun, either. Shock gave way to some kind of masculine relief, for he'd spent most of his days since meeting her filled with such lust toward her, a lust made unnatural because she was a nun.

As he rode back to the estate and anticipated how to tell her of the secret he'd learned, Rurik considered that not much had changed between them. He remembered the way she phrased her words that night at the inn when he was tempted to reveal the depth of his feelings for her.

So, if my vows dissolved on the morrow, there could be no match between us?

His answer still stood…or did it?

Sven was willing to risk his father's good graces for Elspeth, ready to give up his family's wealth and position to marry her. Sven was a second son, his inheritance was modest and he would serve other men for the rest of his life. With his skills and experience, he would never be without a living. As Rurik entered the clearing and passed the two men guarding the entrance, he realized his own truth.

He had lived his whole life with nothing he did not earn and now, when every single thing he hungered for most—name, family, honor, wealth—were almost in his grasp, he could not give it up. So, when he walked into her room and watched her sleep, he knew the answer. Or so he thought.

The sight of the instrument of her deceit on the chair stirred the anger inside him once more and so, when she opened her eyes and gazed up at him, he was furious at her lack of trust. Rather than do something he would regret, he left, planning on speaking to her when his temper cooled over the matter.

And she followed him.

Nay, not only followed him, but put herself within his grasp. What started as a way to show her that she'd been wrong in not trusting him with her honor, fell apart with the first kiss. Instead of fighting him or screaming, Margriet softened under his touch, damning both of them to his lack of control.

He taunted her with her lies, and planned on showing her that he could take them to the edge of bliss and not pass that line. And he could have, had she not moaned in pleasure at his touch and had not her body readied itself to join with his.

Then, at that last moment, when he'd changed his mind and decided to fight for a future together and he'd offered her everything he had, 'twas not his control but her lies that stopped the consummation of his vow.

She carried another's seed in her belly.

Rurik stood some distance from the house now and listened to the sounds of the night, trying to find himself in the maelstrom of his thoughts and wondering what kind of woman would do what she'd done. The owls on watch for mice did not answer him, nor the other predators hunting in the night's air, and he suspected that he would never find it.

She had wanted something to keep them apart and this certainly would. Now, his duty would be done and she would be turned over to her father's mercy and Rurik knew that Gunnar would need every one of his negotiating and planning skills to sort out the problem of his convent-raised, pregnant daughter.

A flickering light caught his attention, moving through the main chamber of the dwelling, and then he spied it in the room above and knew she had made her way back up there. A pang of guilt shot through him as he realized he'd left her tossed about and almost naked on the floor of the larder where she lay when she revealed her secret to him.

He'd fled, something he was not proud of now, because he was not certain of whether to gather her in his arms or to choke the life from her for playing him the fool. Now, out from under passion's insanity, he did not think he would have harmed her, for he'd never raised a hand to a woman other than in pleasure, but then, when her perfidy was revealed at the worst possible moment, he could not be sure.

So, he'd climbed to his feet and walked away.

Rurik gathered his horse and then rode to the guards, giving them orders for the morning. He could not stay here, not in the same house where she was. He would sleep somewhere between here and town and send back one of the men for her.

The ship would leave on the morning's tide and take them all to where they faced their destinies. He cursed himself for being a fool to think, even for a moment, that theirs could have been joined.

Chapter Sixteen

The sun burst through the clouds, and the wind behind pushed them forward on their journey north. For once, the conditions for traveling were favorable and the ship floated smoothly over the waves of the sea. The journey would take them past the island of Háøy, or Hoy as the Scots called it, and on to the mainland and her father's house. They would land near Orphir and travel the last leg on horseback. She knew he'd sent word ahead of their arrival.

Rurik had made arrangements for their travel on a private ship, so 'twas only their men onboard, along with the sailors who guided it across the waves. Even so, she felt as though in the middle of strangers.

A bundle of clothing and terse instructions about readying herself was all that she received this morning, and this from a very sullen Donald, who would not meet her gaze. No words were exchanged on the ride into Thurso, nor on their approach to the harbor. Even her reunion with Elspeth was muted by the events of the night before.

Elspeth explained that she and Sven had ridden straight for the nearest town that had a priest, and one willing to perform the marriage. They were convinced that his parents would not fight a thing already done and Sven was certain of their welcome of her. At that moment, Margriet felt no need to explain how this would not be so, for Elspeth glowed with the aura of a woman in love.

Knowing how she would not have listened to any truth just a few months ago when she thought she was in love, she did not waste what strength she had on a hopeless argument. She did appreciate Elspeth's presence now, and it was thoughtful of Rurik to bring them along, but the desire to talk with someone so very happy fled as she watched him come aboard.

He'd arrived after everyone else was readied for the voyage and, other than a brief word to the captain of the ship and another to Sven, he spoke to no one. Once they'd left the harbor, he'd walked to the front of the ship and stood alone, facing north. Now, about three hours later, he was still there. As she was at the back of the ship, letting the winds swirl around her and soothe her frayed disposition.

If she lived one hundred years more, she would never forget the look of betrayal in his eyes when he discovered that she was breeding. And worse yet, Margriet would always know that that sin now lay on her shoulders along with so many others. It mattered not why she did it, good intentions lay intertwined with sins along the path to Hell as Mother Ingrid would say, it only mattered that she'd brought him to a time when he offered her all that he had, and she rejected it.

No man's pride could suffer that blow and allow him to forgive her. Not even Rurik's intrinsic honor, as she'd come to know him, would allow that. The pain that tore her own heart apart told her she needed to tell him her truth and to release him of any responsibility in what had happened between them, but the distance between them now, greater and deeper than the ocean they traveled on, prevented her from doing that.

As they passed the red sandstone cliffs of Hoy, she knew her time was limited. Soon, they would head east between the islands and towards Orphir. Turning to face the front of the ship, she looked past the censuring expressions of the men to where Rurik was. The wind tore her hair free of Elspeth's attempts to braid it for the voyage, so she gathered it and wrapped it around her fist as she took the first step toward him.

Their disapproval became vocal as she passed and she heard bits and pieces of the explanation given out about why she now dressed not as a nun, but as a noblewoman. It could be worse.

Instead of thinking of them as two silly women, who did not know better than to believe they needed disguises to protect themselves, they could know of her dishonor. Rurik could have told the whole truth

and her shame would now be spreading among them
and like a fire amidst the tinderbox when they set
foot on land.

He protected her even now.

She'd gone only a few paces, balancing against the
rise and pitch of the ship and the winds now at her
back, when Sven discerned her target and blocked her
path.

"Lady, I would caution against approaching him."
He kept his voice lowered so no others would hear
his warning. "He wishes not to speak to anyone."

"I am certain of that, Sven, but it will not stop me."

"Sister…lady," Sven said as he shook his head at
her. "I cannot vouch for…" His words drifted off, but
the fierce frown gave his meaning.

"Sven," she said, laying her hand on his arm, "he
will not hurt me."

"I worry not for you, lady," he answered, concern
for his friend clear now.

"What do you know of this?" she asked. "What
has he said?"

"You know him well enough to know that he
would never say anything," Sven whispered furiously. "But even you, with your short-lived acquaintance of him, would only need to look at him to see
the damage wrought by your lies."

His furor surprised her, for his demeanor had
always been pleasant during the journey, even playing the role of jester among the men. That he should
hold deep emotions should not be a surprise to her

after his chivalric carrying off and marrying Elspeth, but this was.

"'Tis that damage I wish to ease, Sven. Let me pass."

He paused and in that moment, she knew not if he would let her go or not. Then, with a sharp bob of his head, he stepped aside. Margriet's stomach churned now as she walked the short distance to the bow of the ship. Finally, she stood a few paces from him and she tried to think of how to start.

"Sven!" his voice rang out.

Sven pushed around her and leaned in to hear what Rurik said. Some fierce whispering between the two men went on for some minutes before Sven turned and walked away. "I am not your servant, Rurik," he said over his shoulder. "If you want her gone, then make it so."

And still he did not turn to her or say anything. Knowing he would not, she took a step closer and then another until she could have reached out and touched his back…if she dared.

"Rurik," she said, "I…"

"Go away, Lady Margriet," he said without looking back.

"No."

"If you have any sense…" he began.

"Apparently I do not have the sense God gave an ox, according to Donald, that is. Donald has been very clear in his opinion of where women stood in that regard."

"Please, Margriet. Go away," he repeated.

So she said the only thing she could. "No." She did touch him then, placing her hand on the back of his cloak. "I need to tell you the truth, Rurik."

He shrugged her hand off as he would some irritating insect. "I felt the truth last evening, lady. What more is there to say about it?" Now he gripped the edge of the ship.

"If you would listen, I would tell you that I was a foolish girl who believed the first words of love and affection spoken to her in so many years," she said to his back, for he would not face her. "I would tell you that I sinned grievously and knew no way out of it but to lie." Margriet felt the tears flow as she tried to put the words together. "And I would tell you that if I had met a man such as you first, I would have known the difference between love and lust when the challenge came."

The winds whipped around her now as the ship changed directions, but the tears came not from that. The tears came when she realized how stupid she had been to fall for pretty words and attractive promises. She'd given up her body and honor to a man who said the right things, and now she'd bear the price of that failure. And she'd hurt someone deeply who should never have been involved.

"I beg your forgiveness for not trusting you, Rurik, for if I had..." Margriet thought of how this journey could have been, all the consequences of her mistrust and dishonesty and how she had lured Rurik into something beyond their control. "I beg you..."

The sobs welled from deep within and made it impossible to say anything more. She pressed her fist against her mouth, trying to control her despair, and grasped the side of the ship to keep from falling. When she felt she could speak again, she asked, "What will you do now?"

He faced her then, turning toward her but never meeting her gaze as he answered. Instead he stared over her head at the sea. "Complete my duty to Gunnar and then go to my father."

Margriet had forgotten that they were both called back by their fathers. "The prodigal son," he'd called himself.

"What will you do now, Margriet?"

What would she do? She'd thought of nothing else since everything had fallen apart and even more so since she'd fallen in love with him. There was only one thing to do.

"I will tell my father the truth and throw myself on his mercy," she said. "Mayhap he will find Finn to be a suitable husband for me."

Rurik tilted his head and frowned at her. "Finn?" Then his glance dropped toward her belly and he nodded in understanding. "The man…"

But still the frown did not leave his face. They stood looking at each other and she knew this might be the last time she could tell him anything private.

"I pray that you can find it in your heart to forgive me, Rurik. If not now when the thoughts of what I did and how I deceived you are fresh, then mayhap when they fade a bit in your memory."

When he said nothing in reply, she turned and walked to the back of the ship, where Elspeth stood watching her. She could face no one now, so she pulled the hood of her cloak up on her head and bowed her head. Any joy that she should feel upon returning home after so long was dimmed by the pain that tore her apart.

'Twas her penance for all of her sins and she prayed she could accept it as that.

Rurik tried to turn from her and not watch her progress along the deck of the ship, but he failed again, as he did anytime self-control and Margriet were in the same situation. Telling himself it was still his duty to oversee her comfort and safety, he made certain she reached Elspeth's side before turning back to let the sea winds pummel into him. Her words had affected him more than he wanted to admit, but it was the name that bothered him more.

Finn.

Although a common name in Norway and the Orkneys, he knew only one man called that and not by the shortened version of it, but by the whole name.

Thorfinn. His half brother refused to answer to Finn, saying it sounded like a fish's name.

His half brother, who was his father's legitimate son and heir.

His half brother by Erengisl's first wife, who caused his mother's downfall and his own exile to Scotland.

There could be no connection, Rurik knew, because Thorfinn remained at his father's side, secure in the standing and honor that legitimacy gave him. There could be no connection, he told himself again in spite of the warning signs he felt.

Looking to the north and east, he watched as the land of his birth passed them by. The sharp cliffs and mountainous terrain of Hoy, the gentler rolling hills of the mainland, the smaller islands off in the distance.

Their destination was Orphir, the residence of the Earls of Orkney in days long past where his father kept a smaller residence, as did Gunnar. They'd decided that a private reunion would be best considering the many years that separated father and daughter, and it would give Margriet a chance to acclimate herself before being thrown into the life of a courtier's daughter once more. Now, Gunnar had no idea of how wise that decision was, nor did Margriet know.

The winds were with them and the sea was fair, making their voyage a fast one and bringing them to Orphir just before sunset. When they put to port, he sent the men onto his father's house with word of his own arrival. From missives received in Thurso, he knew his father stayed in Kirkvaw while on this visit to the Orkneys from his lands in Sweden. He, too, would take a few days to rest before presenting himself there and entering the mire of arrangements, introductions and preparations that would be his life from this day forward.

He guided Margriet to her father's house alone and with nary a word between them. Rurik could not help but notice that she grew more nervous with each passing minute and realized that she may not remember her father from her childhood.

Although it had been many years for him as well, he did carry the memories of a man who'd been a good friend to him during the difficult times when Rurik's mother fell from his father's grace. One of very few who stood by his side during the ugly mess that ended with him in Scotland and Erengisl married to the old earl's daughter as a favor to his king. The softer personal feelings involved between a man and woman meant nothing where the king was concerned.

"He is a good man, Margriet. You can rely on his judgment," he said as a servant ran out to take hold of their horses and he helped her dismount for the last time.

Her hands shook and she paled with each step forward. Almost to the doorway, she stopped and gazed up at him, a look of complete panic filling her eyes and he feared she would faint dead away.

"I cannot do this, Rurik. I cannot," she said, taking a step back and looking as though she was about to run off.

He took her hands in his and held her steady. When she met his eyes, he repeated to her the first words she'd spoken to him when she acknowledged her identity.

"You are Margriet Gunnarsdottir. Do not forget that."

She took in a deep breath now and nodded at him.

When the door opened and an older man stepped from it, she let her hood fall to her shoulders. Then she walked at Rurik's side to meet the man she did not remember as father. Gunnar shouted at the sight of her, causing tears to stream down Margriet's face.

"I did not expect you to resemble your mother so much, Margriet! You have grown to be a beauty like her. So much like her, my eyes could not believe it," Gunnar said, opening his arms to her. After a brief hesitation, Margriet allowed him to pull her close and hug her.

It was a good start, he thought, as they all entered the house and he watched as Gunnar called out orders for her comfort and told her of his arrangements for her stay there until they visited Kirkvaw. Overwhelmed and surprised, he thought by the warmness of the welcome after such a separation, Rurik knew she would be cared for and knew Gunnar would handle the news of her condition with much wisdom and care.

He stood aside as Gunnar introduced her to his household and she handled things remarkably well for someone about to bolt just a few minutes before. She did glance over at him several times, but less and less as Gunnar brought her back into the place and family she'd been gone from for these last ten years. Gunnar noticed him standing there and came to him.

"I have not yet said how good it is to see you, Rurik."

"And you, Gunnar."

"She has grown so much that I would not know her, but you, you have grown into a handsome man. And so big!" Gunnar was no small man himself, but Rurik did tower over him now, grown at least a foot more since their last meeting thirteen years before. When Gunnar held out his hand, Rurik took it in greeting. "My thanks for delivering her safely into my arms."

"I was honored that you asked me to carry out that duty for you, Gunnar. You were ever a true friend to my mother and me."

Gunnar looked across the room to where his daughter talked with the woman who had served as her nurse. Content that she was getting on well, he smiled. "Does your father know of your arrival yet?"

"I will send word in the morn, Gunnar. I was not certain we would make it here before sunset. How is he?"

"Impatient as ever," Gunnar said, slapping him on the shoulder…the shoulder Margriet had sewn together not long ago. "The many delays have made him on edge, for he'd hoped you would arrive before summer." His father's counselor leaned over and spoke quietly to him. "You know the situation between the king and his sons. Your father agreed to assist in the negotiations before year's end."

"So his letters said."

"He wants you in place before he leaves for Norway." That would explain his father's impatience.

"The delays were not intentional," he said.

"Come now, Rurik. I knew you as a young man. Were you not waiting to be wooed home?" Gunnar laughed now. "That was why I suggested he send the armbands and the sword. Did they not entice you to consider his offer?"

Now it was Rurik's turn to laugh. He should have recognized Gunnar's mark on this, from first invitation to last. "They did, Gunnar. I knew he was serious when the sword arrived for I have never seen it outside his hall in Hultaby."

"As I assured him would be your reaction."

"So, 'tis your hand behind this whole reconciliation then?"

Margriet walked over to them then, ending their discussion, one which would need be finished before he met with his father.

"You know my father well, Rurik?" she asked.

"I knew him as a boy when I lived with my father," he replied. An uneasy feeling moved along his spine as he realized her probable reaction to his parentage.

"And we will be working together on many issues and concerns for your father now that you have returned."

It took about the same length of time for her to recognize his omission as it did for him to understand her sin. But she asked the question anyway.

"You know his father?" she asked, all the while staring at him.

"I have the honor of working for his father, Margriet. You know that I serve Lord Erengisl. And now I will serve Rurik as well."

He remembered wondering if a man's head could explode and now Rurik wondered it about Margriet, for her face grew dark and red and her lips sputtered as she realized the deception played upon her. He'd done it in part to protect her from thinking she was not good enough for him, but 'twas also for his protection, too. Though from her expression, she would not understand that part of it.

Sometimes in battle, the prudent thing was to retreat and fight another day. Thinking that the best course of action, now he bowed to Gunnar and excused himself. Margriet could do nothing now, but he knew she would have her say at some point. Rurik only knew he had some explaining of his own to do to her when that day came.

Chapter Seventeen

Rurik strode down the long hallway on his way to the great room where his father awaited him. Although he would have preferred to have a more informal and less public first meeting than this, he could not avoid it any longer. Messengers had been sent to him in Orphir with an invitation to come at once to Kirkvaw where his father waited on his arrival. When the Earl of the Orkneys sent such a message, no one, not even his son, ignored the summons.

So with Sven and Magnus at his side and his men from Scotland at his back, he walked forward to be welcomed by the same man who'd sent him away nearly ten-and-three years ago. Rurik looked around as he walked and noticed the luxurious, but clean design of the building that was only a few years old. Not like his father's other properties, which demonstrated Erengisl Sunesson's wealth and power, this one fit the city and the islands.

They'd reached the door of the large chamber and stopped, remaining there, as was custom, until being called forward to greet Lord Erengisl. Rurik held his breath, aware that the first stumbling block could be at just this moment. Rising to his full height, he waited for the call. The herald nodded to him as he spoke in a loud voice, one that carried throughout the chamber.

"Rurik, son of Erengisl, come forward."

He could not help the smile that he wore now as he walked forward to accept his father's greeting. So many years had passed, so much yearning laid buried deep inside him for this moment that he feared it might pass too quickly. Several people spoke as he passed by, but he could only focus his eyes ahead, where a large chair sat in the middle of a dais.

And he saw the man in that chair.

'Twould appear that his father aged well, losing none of the vigor he remembered from the last time he saw him. Erengisl sat with authority in that chair and Rurik climbed the steps in front of it, pausing there. Meeting the gaze of his father's deep green eyes, he knelt down and then bowed his head in respect. He remained low until his father rose from the chair and approached him.

Grasping the hand held out to him, Rurik stood and shook his father's hand and accepted in that moment all he offered. After a few seconds, his father pulled him into a backbreaking hold and the hall erupted in cheers at their reconciliation.

When released, Rurik motioned for his friends to

come forward and be presented. Erengisl welcomed them all to his court and his household. Bringing Rurik along onto the dais, Erengisl motioned to a young man at his side and Rurik recognized his half brother Thorfinn.

Although his coloring was that of his mother, Erengisl's first wife, Magnilda, his height and bearing was that of his father. Only a year younger than he, Thorfinn may have carried his noble mother's blood in his veins, but Rurik's mother remained Erengisl's favorite. And that accounted for the lack of warmth in his greeting after these many years.

"Brother," Thorfinn said amiably, although Rurik knew it was only because they were being observed. "Welcome home." He held out his hand in greeting.

How it must have been a bitter taste in his mouth to say those words! Things had ended badly between them when Erengisl decided to marry his present wife, Agnes, at the king's behest, and he put aside Rurik's mother, his mistress of many years. His mother had been the wife of Erengisl's heart, before and even while married to Thorfinn's mother, but marriages for those in Erengisl's class were not based on love or the ability to produce sons—they were based on who gained the most in power or wealth.

And so, with his duty to his liege lord before him and at his demand, Erengisl was forced to give up Moireach and their son. Thorfinn, then only fourteen years old, had cheered the decision, swearing that the Scottish whore's son would never share in their father's inheritance. Now, as he stood side by side with him, Rurik wondered the price of his compliance.

Rurik took the hand offered and shook it. He did not miss the pleased look on his father's face as he did. Apparently, it was important to Erengisl that his sons be reconciled as well.

"So," Thorfinn said, his voice pitched low so that only he could hear it, "the whore's son returns after all."

Rurik felt better knowing the truth and knew he must watch his back. "I thank you for your welcome, brother," he replied, not giving in to the desire to lash out and offer insult to answer insult.

"Come," Erengisl said, waving them along, "I want you to meet those in attendance."

He trailed his father out a door to the side of the dais and into a chamber that served as a meeting place. A group of men followed and took places at the long tables assembled there. Once served wine or ale by servants who stood along the wall, Erengisl introduced them one by one. The only one missing was Gunnar.

"Gunnar joins us on the morrow," his father announced. "Come, Rurik, sit at my side as we discuss the situation of King Magnus." Rurik walked to the seat indicated by Erengisl and noticed that papers already sat there. "Worry not," he said, "Thorfinn will not mind if you sit in his seat while I explain the intricacies of the negotiations."

The glint in his brother's eyes spoke of more than minding giving up his seat of honor, it spoke of revenge for the slight. But once again, his words belied his true feelings, "Of course not, Father. I am pleased to help in any manner possible."

Rurik knew men like Thorfinn. They hid their motives and goals under layers of politeness and carried out their attacks in the dark of night instead of the light of day. You never knew the direction it would come, only that it would happen. He planned on speaking to Gunnar about Thorfinn when the counselor arrived in Kirkvaw.

The discussions proceeded through most of the day, interrupted only by food and wine. Then, at nightfall, they finished and Erengisl invited him to a private dinner. Finally, they would talk as man to man, and father to son. After the public reception and meetings, Rurik admitted that, for the first time, he was looking forward to such a chance to talk with his father. Soon, everyone was gone and only he remained.

"You are not what I expected," Erengisl said as he handed Rurik a cup of wine. "The last memory I have of you is you shaking your fist in anger at me as Gunnar dragged you from my hall."

Rurik remembered the exact moment his father described. His mother had been put aside after being promised marriage and, as her son, he took up her cause. He did not remember his mother asking him to do so, but at that tempestuous age when every wrong look or word is a challenge to honor, Rurik took it up anyway.

"My mother was put aside, after believing your

word that you would have her to wife when Thorfinn's mother died. I remember it well," Rurik said. After drinking some of the wine, he added, "Was it worth it?"

"Your mother understood, Rurik."

"I asked not if she understood, I asked if losing her was worth all you gained in her stead."

At that moment, his father looked aged, the glimmer in his eyes faded and Rurik knew he thought on the question asked…and he thought about Rurik's mother, gone for nigh on ten-and-three years from this island.

"The king demanded the marriage. Agnes would not consent if Moireach lived in any of my houses. I had no choice." His voice lacked the conviction of his earlier conversations and Rurik suspected that the answer he would give, if he could, would be no. "If you still feel that way, why did you return? I ask of you the same that was asked of me—to marry for the sake of an alliance."

Rurik emptied the cup and considered the question and the obvious difference between the two of them. "But I come here with no claims on my heart to accept your offer and the marriage that comes with it."

As soon as the words were let free, he knew them for the lie they were. He nearly laughed at the similarities now between father and son. The difference was that he could not claim Margriet or the child she carried. Something must have warned his father not to pursue the topic, for he ended it with a request.

"Agnes accompanied me on this visit and I would

ask that you show her the respect due a countess…
and my wife. After all, it is her kin involved in the
marriage discussions for you."

Rurik nodded, agreeing to his father's request.
He'd never met the woman—his mother and he being
banished before she would set foot in Erengisl's
home—but this was only a courtesy his father asked.

"So you have grown older and wiser since I saw
you last?"

"Ten-and-six years old is a terrible time," Rurik
offered as an explanation. Now he asked about his
brother. "Tell me of Thorfinn. What is his place with
you?"

"He is never satisfied," Erengisl said.

"That can be a good thing, making him strive for
more or better."

"He earns nothing yet expects it all."

"Father, I would not be the instrument used to
divide you from him." Rurik had thought of this
when he considered the offer made to him. "There is
already enough ill will between us."

"You have indeed grown up, Rurik," he said, rising
from the chair across the table from him. "I have land
enough for my two sons to share, as I did with my
brother. Gunnar has recommended that you take
control of my lands in Sweden and that Thorfinn be
given the Orkneys and my lands in Norway."

"I thought that you had power in name only here,
through Agnes's claim and not blood?"

"Aha! So you have studied it then?" He seemed

pleased that Rurik came here with some knowledge of the situation. "You are correct. Unless Agnes bears me a son, I have no blood claim on these lands, other than that I possess them now and hold them in trust from the old earl through her. But Norway owns these islands and I serve Magnus's and Eric's interests here, so I see no end to my claim, at least not while I'm alive."

Rurik understood his father's plans now, he just did not know if Thorfinn would feel cheated by them. Standing as well, he thanked his father for the meal and excused himself. He'd heard and observed and learned so much today that his head was spinning with it. Walking through the halls, he noticed that servants bowed to him as he passed and the few others still in attendance acknowledged him or stopped to greet him.

A far different situation that when he left sixteen years ago. The thing that worried him most was that with each boon granted him, the desire for more increased. He did not feel greedy about this, he felt as though every dream was being fulfilled for him, everything he wanted was being given him.

There was so much to think about now, his own counselors to choose, and he hoped for Gunnar's thoughts on that. Although he wanted to have Sven and Magnus at his side, he was not as certain about the three men who came from Lairig Dubh. There were most likely others whom his father would recommend, mayhap others due some small reward or honor who should be chosen.

Rurik turned down the final corridor that led to his chambers. It would take some time to learn everything expected of him, but he was committed to this now. His chambers were large and comfortable with a view of the harbor. A servant had prepared his bed, left a pitcher of ale and some bread and cheese on the table and had a fire blazing in the hearth.

He could get used to being treated this way.

"Lady Margriet? Your father is waiting for you and asks you to hasten your preparations." Brynja, the young maid assigned to her care on her arrival at her father's house, stepped into her chambers and delivered the message.

'Twas not about her preparations, for she sat fully dressed and arranged in the new clothing her father ordered for her. With a sigh, Margriet stood, walked to the door and saw her father there in the corridor. He had been patient with her, providing tutors even, to ease her way back into her place here.

They were about to depart for Kirkvaw, for Lord Erengisl had ordered Gunnar and his other counselors and vassals to be in attendance when his son was presented.

His son, Rurik.

Margriet only knew she could not face him without doing something irrational after discovering his lie. And now that she was reacquainting with her father and his family and kin here in the Orkneys, she had no desire to embarrass him with her actions. At least her actions now, for she had not yet revealed the sins of her past to him.

'Twas a near thing, she thought as she walked down the hall to him, for the seamstresses and servants almost discovered the truth when measuring her for the new gowns and tunics. Several tunics pulled tightly across her breasts, breasts now sensitive and sore…and swelling, it seemed, with each day that passed by, and she fought the urge to tear them apart to lessen the pain they caused.

And she'd begun to walk in the most unattractive way, waddling like a duck did. One of the young boys had imitated her as she walked past him and Margriet was stunned by it. Correcting it was another problem of its own, for her hips seemed to ever move like that and no amount of holding her back straight helped.

She was waiting, waiting and giving herself a chance to find Finn to let him know before her father discovered the fact of the pregnancy. She'd even traveled to the market town nearby, hoping to see him there among the merchants, but she did not. And she fought the fear that he was not really there and mayhap not even the person he said he was when they met in Caithness.

Her father motioned to the carts and horses waiting outside and swept her out the door as soon as he took her hand.

"I had forgotten about how much time young women need to primp and prepare themselves for almost any occasion," he said.

"Forgive me for delaying you, Father. If you'd like, you could ride on ahead and I will join you there."

Her father was not a foolish man, but he took her attempt for what it was—nervousness. "And deny me the pleasure of seeing you introduced to Lord Erengisl and his court? Do not think to do it!"

Margriet wanted to cry. Her father had been kind and generous and patient since she'd returned and she would be repaying him with a terrible failure and dishonor. Even as she searched for him, she feared being recognized by Finn before she could confess her sin, for it would mean having her father bear the brunt of it before all those he respected and served. She knew now that in sending her to the convent, he'd thought to protect her during the restless years in Orkney as the old earl died without sons and Erengisl took control in his wife's name. For his concern and love, she would repay him with shame.

Her father had explained how he had urged Lord Erengisl to call Rurik home to prepare him to inherit his father's lands in Sweden. Although Rurik considered himself in exile, his father had kept watch on him and his life since sending him away over a decade ago. At Gunnar's urging, he was called home now to learn from his father and ready himself for the responsibilities ahead.

So when Rurik had said that her father would not approve of him as a match suitable for her, he'd meant that she was beneath him, not above him as she'd thought. For, and the servants were the ones to tell her, Erengisl planned a marriage for him, too. One arranged to his wife's kin that would provide a strong alliance with the royal house of Denmark. Erengisl strove high for his bastard son, mayhap to make up for the years Rurik spent out of favor…?

"Nay, Father, I am but overwhelmed by my journey here and our reunion. Forgive my tardiness."

He helped her into the cart and patted her hand. "There will be time enough for you to rest and become accustomed to our ways here once we are in Kirkvaw." Then he mounted the horse he would ride alongside of the cart so they could talk. "Lord Erengisl has summoned me and we can delay no longer."

"Aye, Father."

The journey to the city would take most of the day, and it left her with much time to think on everything that had transpired between her and Rurik. And one thing that left her puzzled.

At that moment, when he was about to claim her, he knew she was simply Gunnar's daughter and yet he'd offered her everything he had. Was that just to have his way with her or did he mean he would give up his father's plans for her? She was beginning to suspect that men would say anything to gain their pleasure.

Her confusion over him was not aided by the fact that he was all her father talked about since her arrival. Oh, he'd asked the polite questions about the convent, her education, her life there and about the most trivial details of her journey here, but then the topic would change to *him*. Margriet was tempted to laugh when she realized that she was now referring to Rurik as Thora had when she was angry.

Apparently Rurik was everything and more that her father, and his, had hoped for. Even now, as they traveled the road between Orphir and Kirkvaw, he mentioned him again. Finally, she asked the question that had bothered her about this whole arrangement.

"If Rurik has only just returned, how do you know so much about him, Father? Surely, he did not display all this wisdom and good judgment before he was sent away?"

He laughed and shook his head. "I could tell the kind of man he would be when he left, but it took some convincing for Lord Erengisl to believe. And the earl has watched his progress with each passing year as Rurik has become an accomplished warrior and counselor and…"

"Womanizer?"

Her father laughed then, the laugh that men did when appreciating some attribute of another man—part appreciation, part envy and part disbelief. If Rurik was here at this moment, it would have been followed by a slap on the back or a knowing wink from man to man. That much she'd learned while traveling with his company of men. "Well, that as well, it would seem."

She looked at him now in disbelief. "And you trusted him to escort me from the convent even knowing about his reputation with women."

"How did you learn of such a thing, Margriet? Surely not from the nuns?"

"Men talk, Father."

Now it was her father's turn to look at her with an expression of incredulity. "I cannot believe that Rurik would speak of such a thing to you."

Margriet shook her head. "Nay, Father, he did not reveal that to me. The others were not so discreet though."

"Rurik has had his share of…involvements, Margriet, but he is a man of honor. I knew I could trust him with your safety and person."

Her father chose the wrong words, for they brought to mind images of Rurik and "her person," on the floor, wrapped around each other, skin to skin, in the throes of passion. Her breath became short and heat rose within her and she remembered the way his mouth touched—nay, possessed—hers and the way his hand caressed all the places on her body that…that…

"Margriet? Girl? Are you well?"

Her father's voice broke in to her memories of what had happened that night and she touched her face, feeling the heat in her own cheeks now.

"I am but a bit overheated," she said as she tried to think on something else and remove the image of his naked body, all golden skin, all muscle, all male strength, from her thoughts.

Someone called out to her father, which distracted him for the moment. Now, as she thought about that night, *again,* she realized that although she felt as though she was being overtaken by him, much as she felt when covered by the waves of the sea, completely washing over her and dragging her down into mindlessness, she knew Rurik was ever in control. Although filled with anger, so much that it could be felt and smelled, his touch was filled with desire and pleasure. And when that moment came, when she told him to stop, he did.

And that was why she never feared him, even then.

For he had shown himself trustworthy over and over on their journey. When he took notice of her distress while traveling. When he cared for her when she took ill. When he did not repeat the devastating kiss even though she wanted it as much as he did. All showed him worthy of trust. The trust she had given only in part.

Her father attended to other matters and Margriet lost herself in her thoughts for the rest of the day. She broke from her reverie when they approached the city of her birth and she found herself amazed at the changes to it since she'd last seen it.

Even though her memories were that of a child, she could see that it had grown in size and the number of buildings and streets. Still called Kirkjuvágr in Norn by the common folk or Kirkvaw or Kirkwall by the Scots, it was now the central city of the Orkneys and even Earl Erengisl had built a new palace here, not far from the Cathedral of St. Magnus, which rose above the rest of the city. She would stay with her father in the palace since his duties required his constant attendance on the earl and his concerns.

The size of the palace shocked her, for Erengisl

had built it with the usual great hall of Norse castles and added not one, but three towers to that! As they approached it through the main gate, Margriet noticed that even the main part consisted of three floors, one beneath the ground and the great hall with its vaulted ceiling on the top floor. The extent of his wealth was displayed for everyone who visited here to see.

She must have been gaping, for her father laughed now. "Ah, I see you have no memory of this?" She shook her head. "And this is not even his most impressive castle, for that is Hultaby in Sweden."

The cart rolled to a stop and a swarm of servants surrounded them, unloading their belongings and helping her down. Brushing her tunic free of the dust from the roads, she followed them to her father's chambers. Expecting something else, she found he had several rooms together—a sitting room where he could entertain guests, a private area filled with his papers and books and records and two small sleeping areas. Though not each separate rooms, there were areas divided by curtains that hung from ceiling to floor that gave a measure of privacy within each section.

And in the middle of the one she was told would be hers sat a bed. Tempted to climb into it and not come out until morning, she waited for her father's instructions. He'd gone immediately to the earl when they arrived and he came back to his chambers in a state of excitement.

"Come, Margriet," he said, pulling her to her feet while Brynja fussed over her dress and her hair. "Lord Erengisl would meet you now and not wait for morn."

"But, Father," she said. "I look like something just dragged along the road. Can I not prepare myself for such an important meeting?"

Deep inside, Margriet was dreading this moment. Her father had described the earl's ability to discern the truth and not to be put off by appearances, and she feared that, without a father's love to blind him, he would see her truth before she could tell Gunnar.

Her father took her in his arms and held her close. "Fear not, Margriet. He will not find you wanting."

Knowing he would not be dissuaded, she let Brynja make some final adjustment and then she followed her father from the tower where their rooms were located down to the main floor and over to the larger tower where the earl lived. They paused at the doorway while a servant announced them.

After living in an austere convent for the last ten years, the luxury of the earl's chambers nearly overwhelmed her. The floors were covered in costly rugs and the walls displayed huge tapestries that both decorated and conserved the warmth in the room. Shelves held various treasured items such as gold and silver vases and bowls and cups. If she gaped then surely it was her lack of seeing such things at the convent all these years?

"Come, Gunnar, present your daughter to us."

Chapter Eighteen

The order, called out in a loud voice, brought her attention to the two chairs set in front of the large, glass windows on one side of the room. The earl and countess both sat there, watching her as she walked at her father's side. Margriet tried desperately to keep her hips straight as she progressed through the room. Luckily, only a few others stood observing her. When they reached her father's liege lord and lady, she sank in a low curtsy and waited for permission to rise.

The earl clapped his hands, calling for wine for all of them, and Margriet rose as her father guided her to stand. Now looking at the earl and countess, she was surprised at the obvious differences in their ages.

"Welcome to our court, Margriet Gunnarsdottir. I know your father has waited for this moment for a long time and am pleased that it has come."

Erengisl Sunesson's dark green eyes sparkled as he took a silver goblet from one of the servants and

held it out to her. She took it and watched as he also
handed one to the countess at his side. She recognized
his eyes as the same color and shape as his son,
Rurik's. And the nose and the angle of his jaw—all
were traits passed on to his son. Only his coloring was
not, for he had hair the color of the mahogany wood
of his chair and not the pale blond color of Rurik's.

"I would make you known to my wife, Agnes of
Strathern."

Margriet bowed her head to the countess and was
surprised when the woman rose and came to her,
taking her hand and welcoming her into their household. "Welcome, Margriet. I hope you are well after
your long and arduous journey?"

Another surprise, for she would not have thought
that the countess would be apprised of such details.
"I am well, my lady," she replied.

"My husband's son told us of the adversities you
faced along the way here from Caithness," Lady Agnes
said. "And he told us of your resourcefulness in dis-
cerning and treating his men when the sickness came
upon them. I am certain your father is proud of you."

"He did?" she asked, surprised at the countess's
knowledge.

"There he is." The countess waved to someone
behind her, someone she was not certain she was
ready to see again. "Come, Rurik. I was telling Margriet how you told us of her actions when everyone
took ill on your journey."

She'd seen him dressed in the plain garb of a

soldier. She'd seen him dry in the light of day and wet from their fall into the stream. She'd even seen him naked. But nothing had prepared her to see him as he was now—arrayed in the finest clothes, wearing a sleeveless tunic of the finest cloth, with gold armlets and bracelets and a medallion bearing the earl's crest around his neck.

He walked toward her in the way he always carried himself, like a wildcat, poised to lunge at any moment and overpower his prey. He smiled, his eyes catching the lights of the many candles that lit the chamber and his mouth curving into an attractive bow, as he stopped before her. Bowing to the countess first, Rurik then turned to her.

"You look well, Margriet," he said.

She lost her ability to speak then. If she'd thought him pleasing in looks as a warrior, screaming out his name at the convent gates or as a protector when he dove into the water to save her, his appearance now as the nobleman's son was even more so. The tunic was tailored to fit closely and it gave a hint to anyone noticing of the powerful chest beneath it. She knew the look and the feel of that chest.

"Lord Rurik, how goes it?" her father asked.

Giving herself a moment to recover from her surprise at seeing him this soon and from her shallow appraisal of his form, Margriet sipped the wine in the cup and listened to her father question Rurik about his arrival here and his reception so far.

"My father has given me many tasks in this last

day, Gunnar, and I confess I have been waiting for your arrival." He turned his gaze on her and added, "I fear I will have need of your father's counsel in these next days and weeks, Margriet."

No longer did he address her as "lady." She noticed the difference now as a recognition of their differences in standing—he, though bastard-born, now stood above her as daughter of a counselor and landowner. Publicly granted status by his father as one of his heirs, Rurik would be called "lord" by all beneath him.

"He is eager to serve you, Lord Rurik, and has spoken of nothing else to me on our journey here."

She tried, she truly tried not to let sarcasm into her voice, but when he lifted his left eyebrow at her answer, Margriet feared she was not successful. Apparently both her father and the countess sensed that they needed to speak and both fled with excuses of other necessary conversations.

"We should talk, Margriet," he said once they were alone.

"As you wish, Lord Rurik," she answered.

"Margriet, I can explain this…" he began and then stopped when he saw others coming closer to them. Apparently her connection to Lord Rurik and the knowledge that they traveled together from Caithness was now fodder for the gossip that flowed like life's blood through any household.

"Of course, Lord Rurik," she said. She knew he was uncomfortable, but, damn him! he deserved it for lying to her.

He clenched his teeth together and whispered, "Not here. Not now." Then his father approached and she nodded.

"Rurik has told us how you saved his men with your knowledge, Margriet."

"He should be thanking the holy sisters at the convent, my lord. They taught me their healing ways."

"And their modesty as well, 'twould seem." The earl offered the compliment seamlessly and she smiled at his easy manner.

"You honor me, my lord," she answered.

Unfortunately, with the earl's approach and continued questions about her journey and her life at the convent, Rurik found the opportunity to escape. As the evening progressed, they seemed to circle each other, but never did the opportunity to speak come again. When she saw him excuse himself to his father and the countess, Margriet knew it was the chance she needed.

Begging leave from her father and receiving permission from the countess to retire for the night, she left the earl's chambers and ran down the stairs to the main floor. She caught sight of him just as he entered the other tower, where his rooms must be. Following quietly, Margriet reached the stairs when he stepped out in front of her.

"Why are you following me?" he asked, taking her arm and pulling her into the shadows of the stairway.

"You said we should speak, Lord Rurik. I but obeyed your command."

"Come," he said, shaking his head as though not certain he should.

He looked over her head and raised a finger to his lips, cautioning her to quiet. The sound of footsteps somewhere behind her trailed off and then there was silence. Rurik took her hand and led her up to the second landing. Once there, he guided her to his chambers. When the door closed, he faced her.

"So, Rurik, Erengisl's son, 'twould appear that you kept secrets, too."

His gaze went to her belly and she put her hand there on the growing swell of it. Instead of reacting in anger at her challenge, he sighed and walked to the window. Staring out, the stark wanting in his voice when he spoke startled her.

"Have you ever wanted something so much that it was like a hunger in your belly, Margriet?" He paused, but she knew he did not want an answer. "And you were willing to give up everything you had and pay any price for that which you craved?"

He could not have known that he described her seemingly starving need for love and the consequences of being so needy. Yet, his words confirmed every emotion in her during those last years at the convent—wanting to belong and be wanted and be needed…and be loved.

"I lived here before. Here and at the earl's castles in Sweden and his estates in Norway. Wealth was never a question when I was a child. Bastard-born or not, Lord Erengisl provided for my mother and me. Any request was granted. Any possession bought or given us." He glanced at her then, for a moment and then away again. "But what I wanted more than any of the things was his acceptance and his name," Rurik said.

And his love, she added silently, knowing now that they both wanted and needed the very same thing.

"When my father banished us," he continued, "I lost it all and, even though the MacLeries welcomed me, the longing never went away."

"And now you have a chance to claim all that you have ever wanted?" she asked, already knowing his answer.

His eyes were bleak when he faced her now and as he walked toward her, she could feel the terrible choice he needed to make.

"He's been watching me all this time. Watching and waiting to see if I am the kind of man he can leave in his stead, Margriet. His summons, even if at your father's urging, meant he believes in me. The answer is aye, I am worthy."

"Rurik, you were always worthy," she began to argue.

"Your words cannot change my past, my beginning," he said, a sad smile flitting across his features, softening them for a moment and revealing a vulnerability she'd not seen before in him. "In many ways, I think you were the last test for me."

"How so? Do you think I am in league with your father? That I was sent to tempt you from all you desire?" She was offended by his words, but then realized he did not mean that she intentionally tested him.

"Oh, I think you are temptation in its purest form, lady, and I think the Fates sent you to me. They gave me one last reason to turn from my destiny, and gave me the best one last."

Pain shot through her as she came to understand that they were not the same after all—love meant all to her and nothing to him. She needed to leave before she embarrassed herself and begged him for his love as she'd begged Finn. No matter his answer, it could not give her what she sought much as he sought his fortune and future here. Neither outcome would be the right one. Margriet grasped the latch on the door and lifted it, her hands unsteady as she opened it.

"And I thought we were the same, Rurik, but now I see how very different we are after all." She leaned her forehead against the door and whispered the rest. "You have love in your grasp and would sacrifice it for everything you desire and I sacrificed everything for the love I thought within mine. I just know not which of us was the bigger fool."

"Margriet, I am sorry," he said from behind her. "I cannot…I cannot…"

She held her hand up to stop him. The excuse mattered not, only his answer to her unspoken question. And now she had it. The rest of her journey would be alone, she knew that now. Finn was like some figment of her imagination, making her face her weakness and leaving her with the consequences.

"You should speak to your father soon," he said. "Before anyone tells him. Gunnar is an honorable man and will help you."

That moment was not one when he should be offering advice, especially when it was about how she would live without him. Margriet ran out of his chambers and down the steps, turning into the great hall…and slamming right into someone. The man grabbed hold of her shoulders and kept her from stumbling to the floor.

"Your pardon," she began to say as she regained her balance and stepped back. "I was rushing and not looking."

Keeping her face tilted down, for she really did not want to answer questions about why she was leaving Rurik's chambers, she pulled from the man's grasp. "My thanks for your help, sir."

"'Twas my pleasure, my sweet," he answered.

At first she knew he must think her a harlot visiting Rurik, but the voice was too familiar. She did not dare to stop as she tried to remember which of the men in their company of travelers had that tone. 'Twas not Donald, for his voice tended to go high, and Leathen's was deeper than this one. Sven and Magnus had the right accents, but 'twas neither of them.

Margriet reached the other side of the chamber when she realized the truth. Glancing back, she caught sight of the man, still standing where she'd left him. The distance was large and the candles threw only a dim light, but she could see his face.

His beard was gone now and his hair was longer, but it made no difference. Margriet was certain of his identity. For some reason she could not define, instead of running to him, she ran away.

Hoping he had not seen her face, she made it to her father's chambers, checking several times to reassure herself that he did not follow her. When she reached her bed, she climbed into it without undressing and pulled the blankets up to cover her. Her stomach heaved and she thought she would be ill, but she lay still and tried to calm herself.

Finn was here! He'd not lied; he was here in Kirkvaw waiting for her arrival. Did he recognize her?

Although in some ways this comforted her, in more ways it unnerved her, for now her father would find out the truth and her fate would be sealed. Judgment day was here for her and after all of her hoping and praying, she had no idea of what would happen.

He'd been truly surprised by her, running down the stairs that led to his half brother's chambers. Thorfinn had been watching her since she arrived earlier this day, but did not want to expose her yet. He needed to make certain that Rurik had a good taste of his "new life" before Thorfinn ripped it from his hands and sent him back to where he belonged. For now, he watched as she staggered away from him and he could tell she was not certain of his identity yet.

Aye, he'd changed his appearance somewhat, shaving the beard he wore when he met and ruined her, and letting his hair grow back to the length he preferred, but still, he would think she would recognize the first man she let into her body. Especially when she swore her undying love for him as he pushed into her, pummeling her virtue and her honor with one thrust.

She was just as much a whore as the rest of them, swiving so many that she remembered none. He suspected that she'd let Rurik have her as well, for his spy reported that an incident had happened between them outside of Thurso to him and he had no doubt that his half brother would take what she offered. The fact that Rurik took her on the floor and left her there when he finished just proved that they both deserved each other.

Though he himself had been her first, she would be fit for no one else when he finished with her, or mayhap he would share her with many, he had not decided yet. The bastard she carried in her belly, for he felt the hardness there when their bodies collided, was of no consequence to him and would more than likely not survive his plans for her. It worried him not, for in that he was better than his father before him who indiscriminately spread his seed, allowing his whore to bring forth his bastard. Thorfinn would not let that happen.

He heard the steps of someone approaching and waited for Rurik to find him there. How touching! He followed her, probably panting after her and wanting more.

"Brother," he said in greeting, though the very word burned his mouth with its insult. "Was that Gunnar's daughter I just saw?" Rurik hesitated in his answer, so he urged him on. "Sigurd pointed her out to me when she arrived earlier."

"Aye, it was."

He raised his brow and demanded an answer with just that simple gesture…and he got it.

"We needed to talk."

"Ah, talking with Gunnar's daughter," he said, with all the sincerity he could muster. "The two of you must have much to talk about." He paused just long enough and then added, "You both being newly arrived and strangers to most here, of course."

Rurik nodded at his words and, with a curt farewell, he climbed back up the steps to his chambers, his pursuit of the slut interrupted for now.

So when questioned about this, he could truthfully say that he saw Margriet coming from Rurik's chambers in the middle of the night and Rurik, man of honor that he was, would have to corroborate his words…and damn them both. Thorfinn laughed to himself at the ease with which some were led to slaughter.

One of Rurik's biggest problems was that he needed to learn that there was only one use for a woman's mouth…and it was not talking. 'Twas a lesson those who served him knew well, as would Margriet in due time.

Chapter Nineteen

Five days had passed since Margriet came to his chambers and he'd not seen her since. He followed her to deny her claim about them, but when he found Thorfinn returning to his own chambers, he decided against it. Torn between finally accepting that there could be nothing between them and begging for her to accept the love he had for her, he took her disappearance as her answer.

Now he'd traveled with his father and Thorfinn to their outlying properties near Birsay and learned more about their interests in and ownership of several businesses in Kirkvaw. Their fishing boats made up half of those who fished the waters off the main islands here and their grain counted as more than one third of all grain leaving for Scotland and Norway. Erengisl would remain a very wealthy man on just his income here alone.

Erengisl also introduced him to one of Lady

Agnes's kin who was also kin to Denmark's king. Lady Ingeborg was lovely and demure and respectful and wealthy and of royal blood—everything that Margriet was not—and he found himself hoping she would wink at him or question something he said or refuse his request, anything but comply with unceasing politeness. After spending a few hours in her company, Rurik knew she would never do anything unseemly, such as disguise herself as a nun or purposely fall into a river because she was too hot. Or follow him when he was in anger's grasp.

But she would, after all the negotiations were finalized, become his wife and mother to his children. When he thought of it in that way, his life stretched out before him with every possibility of him being bored to death by her, for Ingeborg would be the perfect wife for Erengisl's son.

Over the next days, Rurik was invited to the homes of a few of the more important merchants and each tried to impress him with their wealth and generosity, gifting him with horses, silver and even a few servants. The most surprising gift was presented one night when he stayed with the merchant who ran two market towns for his father and was in charge of importing cattle and other livestock to the islands.

He would have expected to receive several heads of cattle or some newly butchered pigs or goats, but instead Rurik opened the door to his room just before dawn to find the man's daughter there, naked but for the ribbons and jewels in her hair. At first he thought her lost or confused or mayhap even drunk, but when he looked out into the corridor, both the merchant and his wife stood waiting expectantly for him to accept her.

Once he thanked them and refused their gift, though not their good wishes, he realized the lesson in it—some would do anything to win the favor of Erengisl and his sons. Even giving their daughters to him for bedplay.

He had never had a problem finding a woman when he had the need or desire when he lived in Scotland, but his change in circumstances brought them out in droves to his door, the corridor outside his door and even into his bed when one enterprising young woman bribed a servant to allow her in. The servant and the woman were dismissed.

He found himself out of sorts with no desire to bed those he initially found appealing. Each time he kissed them or touched them, he found himself comparing them to Margriet and her reactions to his kiss and his touch. Desire fled then and he slept alone.

By far, the most bizarre occurrence happened in Thorfinn's chambers when he answered his brother's invitation for the noon meal and instead was met by a serving girl barely ten-and-five who began to undress him while he waited for Thorfinn's return. When he stopped her from removing his tunic and breeches, she tried to touch him through them. Finally, he held her apart from him and she dropped to the floor, begging him to let her pleasure him or to kill her for she did not want to face her master if he found she disobeyed his orders.

The situation shook him to his core, for never had he threatened any woman into pleasuring him nor harmed any during his amorous adventures, no matter how ardent the loveplay became, and he would not begin now. When he took the girl by the arm and she cried out in pain, Rurik peeled back her tunic and discovered lash marks all over her body. The sight turned his stomach and he took her to Gunnar with orders to keep her safe until he discovered the truth of it.

Thorfinn, it seemed, also took pleasure in demeaning those less powerful and those under his control. Had he expected Rurik to be pleased by the girl's attentions? Who had whipped her and why? He would investigate more and then have words with Thorfinn, for he was certain their father did not countenance such cruelty to servants.

But before he could speak to Thorfinn, he received a summons to his father's chambers to share the evening meal. When he arrived, Thorfinn was complaining that he had yet to meet Gunnar's daughter and asked Erengisl to invite them to the gathering. Apparently Margriet had been ill these last few days and had kept to her father's rooms. Although Gunnar tried to talk his way out of calling her there, Thorfinn insisted and, with Erengisl's approval, sent word for her to come.

Something was not right in all this, but Rurik

could not reason it out. A short time later, Margriet arrived and Erengisl invited her forward to meet his other son. He'd never seen her so hesitant before and he watched from his seat as Gunnar escorted her to his father. The countess came around the table and took her hand, drawing her closer to his brother.

"I am certain that you are not used to our ways yet after so many years in the convent, Margriet, but we prefer to dine together in good company. I am glad you could join us after feeling poorly these last few days."

"I thank you for your kindness, lady. I am certain I will become accustomed to the festive meals you offer in your household."

"Now, come and meet my husband's older son, Thorfinn."

As Rurik watched what happened, he swore that time slowed, for everyone moved at a sluggish pace, making it even harder to bear. Margriet's head jerked back as the countess called his brother over to be introduced and she lost every bit of color in her face. Margriet began to shake her head and back away, stopped only by her father behind her. Then, as his brother reached out to take her hand, she collapsed at Gunnar's feet.

The chamber erupted into chaos at that point and everyone seemed to move faster now. Gunnar bent over to try to lift Margriet, but Rurik got there first and carried her to a couch at Lady Agnes's direction. The countess waved everyone back as she dabbed at Margriet's face with a dampened linen. After a few minutes, Margriet opened her eyes and spoke a name, a name that would damn her.

"Finn?"

Lady Agnes frowned and shook her head. "Do you mean Thorfinn, Margriet?"

Margriet struggled to sit up as she sought the face that had sent her into a faint. Searching one to the next, she found him, standing across the room. "Finn," she said again, waiting for him to acknowledge her.

"I have not heard that name for some time," Lord Erengisl said. "It was a pet name used by his mother." The earl met her gaze and said, "He prefers Thorfinn now."

He walked over to her, smiling now, and she knew her worries were over. But with his first words, they began anew.

"Sweet Peggy? Is that you?" Finn said, shaking his head as he lifted her chin and looked more closely at her. "Gunnar? I thought you said this was your daughter?"

"Why are you pretending that you do not know me?" she asked, the horror growing within her as she realized he did this apurpose.

"Oh, I knew you, I knew you well," he said with an expression that told the others that he was as surprised as they were. "I just knew not that you were Gunnar's daughter."

Her father took his bait, and she wanted to die inside as he stumbled into this fray without being warned first. "Here now, Lord Thorfinn. You insult my daughter without cause. You are mistaking her for someone else."

Finn laughed suggestively and shook his head. "She called herself Peggy when she spread her legs for me."

Margriet did not think, she simply reacted. Jumping up from the couch, she ran at him and slapped him as hard as she could. She never saw the back of his hand as he returned her blow, knocking her off her feet once more.

When Rurik saw her go down again, this time because of Thorfinn's blow, he leapt over the couch and grabbed his brother by the throat. "Do not lay a hand on her again, Thorfinn." Tightening his grip, he pressed harder until his brother choked and sputtered, and until his father stepped in and pulled him free of Rurik's grasp.

"I do not understand how this happened, Father," Thorfinn gasped. "I met her on Lord Kenneth's lands when I went to take your trade offer to him and your cousin, Lord Alexander." Rurik watched as he took a step back, one that placed their father between them and one that protected the weasel's sorry arse from his reach. "You know how peasants are, offering their favors for a few coins or a trinket. She offered hers— I paid her when I finished."

Lady Agnes gasped at his crudity and looked to her husband to take control. He turned to find Gunnar sitting ashen-faced at his daughter's side. Erengisl ordered the room cleared of everyone but the six of them, but Rurik knew that, even now, the news spread through the palace about Gunnar's daughter. There was no way to stop it, but Rurik needed to try.

"Father, these are serious claims made against Gunnar's honor. We should wait until Margriet is able to answer questions before allowing Thorfinn to continue to besmirch her reputation."

Thorfinn did the most unexpected thing then—he laughed long and loud, until tears poured down his cheeks. The display even disturbed Erengisl, who called out to him.

"Thorfinn! Truly this is no time to make light of Rurik's suggestion. If the things you say are true, Margriet is ruined as well as Gunnar."

"But, Father, 'tis amusing when a man who used her during their journey would defend the whore's honor. He even took her on the floor of Old Einar's house outside Thurso when they stayed there."

Rurik did not remember covering the distance between them now, but it took three of his father's guards to wrench him off Thorfinn's throat and hold him from another attack. Only the sight of Margriet's bruised face and his father dragging Thorfinn aside and whispering furiously to him stopped Rurik from lunging again.

"Father, call a physician to see to her," he shouted over the uproar. "She has been ill." He did not dare reveal the rest of it at that moment, though he did not doubt it would be discovered shortly.

Erengisl pushed Thorfinn into a chair and ordered a guard in front of him. Then he walked to Gunnar's side, leaned in and spoke to his counselor quietly so that none but those two could hear. Gunnar nodded, accepting whatever his father said, and then Erengisl sent a guard off with a gesture to find the physician.

Lady Agnes, the only one who remained calm during this situation, remained at Margriet's side until the healer arrived.

"My lord, with your permission and her father's, I would like to examine her," the man said. At his father's nod, two guards picked her up and carried her to one of the smaller alcoves for privacy. A servant who'd accompanied him into the chambers ran out after receiving instructions to bring back certain supplies, no doubt.

Only then did Rurik think about the progress of this debacle and could he see the way Thorfinn orchestrated it. He knew Margriet the first night she'd arrived here, so his surprise and claim to not have known rang false. Unfortunately, his other claims were most likely true. Once more, a wave of warning pulsed through him as he realized that someone was feeding information to Thorfinn about what happened on their journey.

Soon, he heard Margriet stir and heard the healer asking her some questions and he knew that at least she was conscious. And now he waited for the rest of Thorfinn's manipulations with no way to warn Margriet of what was coming. First the healer called Lady Agnes behind the curtain that separated them and then she bade Gunnar enter as she left.

Rurik knew the news she would share now with her father and did not envy his old friend the shock of it. He only hoped that he was right in his belief that Gunnar would help and not hurt her when all was done and said.

Margriet held the cold cloth against her face, trying to soothe the bruise there from Finn's blow, but nothing would be able to ease the pain she would deliver to her father now. He allowed Lady Agnes to pass and then came to sit at her side.

"Father," she whispered, "I beg your forgiveness for shaming you so."

He reached out and touched her other cheek, pushing her hair back out of her eyes, kind even in the face of her shame.

"It is true then, Margriet? You laid with him as he said?" His voice shook, too, as he asked and she felt the hot burning tears pour from her eyes.

She was tempted to turn away in that moment, but she owed him more than that. "It did not happen as he said, but, yes, Father, I gave my virtue to him." The despair on his face and the way he ran his hand through his hair tore her heart open in her chest. "I thought myself in love, Father. A sad excuse, but my only one. He promised me marriage, promised me his name and I believed him."

"But you were in a convent. How did he take your virtue if you were in a convent?"

She tried to explain but it was too hard to form the

words and speak them. Her throat was tight and her chest heavy as she attempted to make him understand, but none of that mattered now, for she had failed him and destroyed his honor by her mistake. Finally, she could speak and she told him how she met him.

"I was out with some of the sisters gathering herbs in the forest near the convent and saw him riding past. I'd lived with the holy sisters for ten years and had never really met or talked to any man younger than Iain, our shepherd. I just wanted to talk to him and find out about the world outside the convent, Father. Truly."

She took his hand in hers and kissed it. "I failed you, Father. I surrendered the only thing I had of value and have ruined you with my mistake."

His eyes filled with tears, too, and then he took her in his arms and held her. "Ah, my girl, we can find a way out of this."

She cried harder at his words, for they meant more to her than anything at this moment. But she feared he would not be as forgiving when he discovered the rest. For a daughter ruined like she was could find haven in a convent or even a marriage to someone who would accept her as damaged goods, but the bairn she carried changed all of it, in more ways than she could even think of right now.

And she had yet to tell him. He released her and started to stand when she held him fast. "I fear this is not something easily put aside, Father." She let him go, but took his hand and placed it on the swelling of her belly. She knew when he understood, for he wore the same expression of horror and betrayal that Rurik had when he discovered the truth.

But that look was nothing compared to the utter disappointment in his gaze when it finally met hers. He stared at her as though she were the worst sort of criminal, guilty of any number of crimes. For so many years, all she longed for was her father's love and now she had forfeited that by her actions.

"Father, I am…"

He pulled away from her before she could finish and walked out of the alcove, opening the curtain and exposing her to the curious stares of those in Lord Erengisl's chambers.

"The girl says she carries your child, Lord Thorfinn. What say you to that?"

Chapter Twenty

The quiet that had reigned in his father's chambers now broke as Thorfinn chuckled and Rurik was seized with the urge to go after him again. And he would have, had not the guards taken up their positions when Gunnar returned.

The man's face was like stone, hard and gray, as he approached his brother with the accusation. However, the expression that no one seemed to notice but him was Margriet's. For as Gunnar called her "girl" and not daughter, she crumbled.

He turned away now, trying to figure out Thorfinn's motives in ruining Gunnar and his daughter, and could think of none. He did not doubt that the journey to visit his father's kin was deliberate and meant to offer him the chance to "find" her. And remembering how deceitful he was as a child, turning from vicious to fair when in his father's view, he also did not doubt that he had seduced her with soft words and promises.

As she'd told him, or tried to tell him, and he would not listen.

Thorfinn shrugged in response. "It could be mine or it could be any man she swived before or after me, Gunnar."

Everyone was so intent on his words, they never noticed Margriet leave the alcove. Rurik watched now as she staggered over to Thorfinn. "That is a lie. Lord Erengisl…Father…I was pure…untouched before I laid with Thorfinn."

"Pure, Margriet? Untouched? Do you mean like a nun would be? The kind of nun you pretended to be on your journey home to cover your secret as long as you could?"

Somehow, Thorfinn managed to take a grain of truth in everything he described and twist it into something else completely. Rurik was done with this now, and called out. "Father, let me explain."

When the guards did not release him fast enough, he broke their hold and tossed them aside. Instead of heading for his brother, he walked to his father's side and spoke directly to him.

"She thought only to protect herself and her young maid on the journey. The lady was among strangers and sought the shelter a religious habit would give them until she felt safe. Even the reverend mother from her convent sanctioned her action."

"The reverend mother knew your reasons for pretending?" Erengisl asked her.

Margriet wavered in her answer. "She knew I needed protection, my lord."

Rurik knew Thorfinn would grab on to any prevarication and use it. He closed his eyes and prayed she would admit the truth so Thorfinn could not make use of it against her.

"But she did not know I was carrying a child."

"And you claim the child is Thorfinn's?" Erengisl asked her quietly.

Rurik turned and watched as she spoke the words. "Aye, my lord. He fathered the child I bear."

As though all her strength left her, she stumbled then. Gunnar reached out to steady her, but then drew away and she was left to her own means then. He could not stand to watch her struggle any longer and since Gunnar had abandoned her, Rurik went to her side, holding her up with his arm around her waist.

"You deny the child is yours, Thorfinn?" their father asked. Now that he held on to Margriet, the sad excuse for a man felt safe enough to leave his chair.

"It could be, Father. It could be any man who passed through that area and who had a few coins to spare."

He held her fast, whether to keep himself or her from attacking his brother, he knew not, but either way, Thorfinn was safe for the moment.

"I can see that you do not believe me, but ask my brother. Ask him if he knew she was breeding. Ask him if they did not act like two dogs in heat during their journey, he sniffing at her while she opened her legs for him. For all I know, it could be his bastard she breeds in her belly and not mine at all."

Rurik said nothing, but Thorfinn pressed on this issue.

"Did you lay with her? Could it be yours?"

Oh, he was good at this, Rurik thought, but he could not lie in this regard. "Nay, I did not."

He must have spent many hours weaving the lies so he was ready when the opportunity arose. Margriet sagged against Rurik and he could tell she was weakening.

"You have woven quite a tale, Thorfinn. A master weaver to be sure," he said. "You make claims you cannot prove to ruin her. But why? Why play this hand at all?" Rurik thought to force him to the truth, but he felt the trap spring as he asked the question.

"To the contrary, Brother, I would take her to wife and clean the stain from her honor if she would have me. I know how much a trusted friend Gunnar is to our father and would marry her if he wished me to do so."

He felt and heard Margriet's gasp at Thorfinn's words. He was certain, from even the little she had told him, that she'd loved the man he pretended to be when he seduced her. Now though, seeing the true man behind the mask, she would never consent.

"You seem so convinced that I lie about her behavior, making your own accusations against me. Mayhap you would like the chance to save her from dishonor and marry her yourself, even though you have said it is not your child?"

All it took was some inattention on his part, a missed clue, and the quicksand opened at his feet. Though Rurik now saw the motivations behind the manipulations, he'd stepped right into the trap. This was about ruining him as much as ruining Margriet and her father.

Even knowing that, he could not give the answer he wanted to, for in that moment, he knew it was a choice between a woman he loved and everything else he'd ever wanted in his life. The acceptance of his father's offer of a name and family and all that he'd lost years ago restored, all that stood in the balance now against Margriet's love.

It was the worst moment in his life and it seemed to stretch on forever. He knew in his heart that he needed to protect Margriet, and he could have sworn that it was only a momentary pause, but when she faced him with sad acceptance on her face, Rurik knew that it had been too long.

"Margriet," he said as she pulled away from him. "Wait."

He wondered if he was looking into a mirror now when her expression collapsed and he knew she felt betrayed. "I understand, Rurik. Truly I do," she said in a desolate voice.

"Father, this has been unpleasant enough. Can we finish the arrangements in the morning?" Thorfinn asked, an unrecognizable sincerity in his voice now that he'd won. At their father's nod, he turned to his stepmother. "Lady Agnes, would you see to my betrothed?"

Rurik watched as the countess and the physician assisted Margriet from the chamber. He shuddered as he had a premonition that the worst was yet to come.

"Gunnar, I will not take responsibility for a bastard when I do not know if it even mine. So, no marriage will take place until she whelps it. What you do with it, if it survives at all, is your concern and not mine."

Rurik turned then and walked away without looking back.

The fog that rolled in before dawn and covered the castle in an impenetrable layer only signified the mood of many of its inhabitants. Especially his. Rurik had walked the battlements all through the night and could tell anyone interested the exact moment when the fog appeared and moved into place.

When morning came, and it was difficult to cipher due to the fog, he went to see Gunnar, to try to convince him not to accept Thorfinn's explanations or offer of marriage. He found empty chambers and a servant said they'd left before dawn for his estate in Orphir.

He went to his father and tried to reason things out with him, sharing his suspicions about Thorfinn with him to no avail. Without proof, there was no way he could answer the accusations and at the bottom of it all lay the truth—Margriet surrendered her virtue to him and now carried his child. Rurik knew there was proof somewhere, he just could not figure out where it was.

Unfortunately, he had no standing in the matter, so trying to break any betrothal would fail. Loving the woman promised in marriage to his brother was not a legal reason in the eyes of the church. Rurik had admitted in front of all of them that there was no chance the child was his, so he could not even claim that right. And, there was his own betrothal, being finalized within days, to consider. Soon, the locks would turn on all of the chains and there could be no freedom.

Since the foul weather matched his foul mood, he gathered twelve of the guards and battled them one after another until none could move. Exhausted but now clear-minded, as battle tended to make him, he finally realized who among his men had been working against them and giving Thorfinn the information— even the truth of things—that had been used to bait and spring the trap. When a servant brought news of a body discovered in the middens outside the castle, Rurik knew how he could prove it and hopefully find a way to put a stop to any marriage between Margriet and Thorfinn.

His men entered his chambers a short time later, all silent, for most knew what had happened last evening. Most every inhabitant of the castle and the town knew, for when one of the highest fell from grace, some gloated, some celebrated, some mourned, but they all knew. Gunnar had long been in his lord's favor and he'd made enemies over the many years for counsel given and recommendations made or opinions held. Thorfinn was not the only one who wished disgrace upon him.

Rurik stood before them and looked from one to the next as he spoke. "You know what happened last night and I am here to find out the name of the man who helped Thorfinn perpetrate this attack on Gunnar's honor."

"What do you mean, Rurik? Do you think one of us a spy for him?" Sven asked.

He could feel their indignation rise at his statement, but he nodded anyway. "Aye. One of you has been helping Thorfinn from the beginning. The delays in receiving my father's summons. Thorfinn's accidental meeting with Margriet near the convent. The tainted meat that took us ill. Someone even followed me back from Thurso and reported on what happened between Margriet and myself."

Some angry muttering began among them, but no one admitted anything. He approached the canvas-wrapped bundle on the floor and untied the cords holding it closed. As he unrolled it as gently as possible, he watched their faces for some sign of their recognition and guilt.

"The guards found her body in the middens this morning."

To a one, they grimaced at the sight before them. He looked from one to the next as he explained.

"My brother's handiwork, or his man Sigurd's. He sent her to me to offer me pleasure, but I refused. I do not use children. When she begged me to kill her rather than make her face his displeasure, I took her to Gunnar for safety. Thorfinn must have found her there when he went to discuss the marriage contracts."

He knelt down and pulled the canvas sheet back around the battered and bruised body, covering her from their sight. It mattered not, for he knew the memory of how the girl died would be with them forever and more so for him, as it was his failure to protect the girl that led to her death.

"This," he said, pointing at the bundle as he rose to stand, "is the fate meant for Margriet Gunnarsdottir."

"Nay!" cried the one who'd betrayed his trust. "He did not kill this girl."

"Do not believe his lies, Magnus. You saw her. You saw the marks from his whips on her back and legs. He left his signet ring on to make certain I knew it was him."

"Rurik," Magnus began, but Rurik stopped him, dismissing the others before continuing.

"I care not that you chose my brother over me, but I will not stand by and let him do more harm to Margriet, Magnus."

"He will not, Rurik. He said he's pleased now that he will receive a huge dowry, for your father is adding to whatever Gunnar pays to make it worth his while."

That was something he did not know. More money meant more reasons to make certain the marriage did not last very long. It meant Margriet was in even more danger than he first thought.

"You will not act against him even for her?"

"Our bond goes back years, Rurik. You would not understand. Thorfinn and I have both been displaced by…" Magnus paused then, realizing he probably did not want to finish his explanation.

"Bastard sons returned." Rurik finished it for him.

It always came down to class. A bastard son, no matter how accomplished and brave, was never worthy enough for those born legitimately.

"I can do nothing to protect her, Magnus. I ask only that you inform me if you begin to suspect I might be correct. Simply send me word and I will see to her safety."

Magnus did not agree, but he turned and, with a silent glance at the bundle on the floor between them, left the chamber. Rurik prayed that he had gotten through to the man he thought his childhood friend.

Days passed and Thorfinn wisely walked a wide path around him, not even appearing at meals or meetings. Gunnar remained at Erengisl's side, but showed no enthusiasm for business or negotiating or any of the tasks that made him an asset to the earl. The cloud of dishonor would hang over his head until the marriage was accomplished and that would not happen for months.

Thorfinn had effectively neutered his most vocal opponent and Rurik knew it was but a matter of time before his brother began to use his newfound strength of position to his advantage. Some of those recently vying for his favor now knocked at his brother's door with their offers and gifts. Knowing that his own marriage would take him from these islands, these men were not fools and knew who would control things here after Erengisl.

Three weeks after Margriet's disgrace had been exposed, Rurik returned to his chambers to find a one-word message left on his bed.

Now.

Chapter Twenty-One

The day had dawned clear, unlike so many lately, so Margriet begged leave to walk on the shore. She was not exactly a prisoner, but she not did have the freedom to come and go as she pleased. Her betrothed husband sent directions for her care and made it clear to the men and women left in charge of her the price for failure if anything happened to her.

She threw her cloak over her shoulders and walked to the ruins of the old church at the end of her father's estate. The winds blew strong but not too cold yet, and she enjoyed the bite of it. When she reached the piles of rocks, for that was all that was left now of the circular church dedicated nearly two centuries ago to Saint Nicholas, she sat and let the sun beat down on her.

Her maid Brynja had been replaced by an older woman who did not like to walk and who began complaining within minutes of leaving the house. Margriet ignored her as long as possible because her walks were one of the few pleasures left now that her life had fallen apart. Oh, she did not downplay her part in her own failures, but she wondered if this was her penance or if it had not yet begun. On thinking about that question and about the real Thorfinn, who was only now showing himself to her, she thought it had not yet started.

Finally when the woman's nagging ruined the beautiful day, Margriet turned and headed back to the house. She paused to watch some boats pass by close to shore. Seeing them now always made her wonder about Rurik.

She could not—nay, indeed, did not—blame him for the way things worked out. He'd been honest with her about his dreams and his need for the things his father offered him. And when the question was put to him, when he could have done more good by lying, he told the truth. He chose everything he'd wanted in his entire life over love.

Pushing her hair out of her face, she watched as the larger ship sailed on past the docks and a smaller one turned to maneuver into place there. It seemed like a lifetime ago when she'd arrived here to return to her father's home, hoping to find compassion and the truth. Oh, she'd found the truth, but it was not what she had hoped for.

She did not matter.

Not to her father, who exiled her for ten years and then abandoned her when she caused his honor a blow.

Not to her betrothed, who only wanted the obscenely large dowry that Erengisl was providing to soothe the insult to his honor.

And not to the man she foolishly fell in love with.

That hurt the most, in spite of knowing he'd warned her of the choice he would make, and in spite of knowing that she'd damaged his pride and betrayed his trust, several times in just the short time since they'd met.

She sighed then, a signal to Aslief to begin complaining about her dawdling again. She turned and followed the path back to the house, knowing that one long day would lead to another and another, and nothing could change the situation.

She did not matter to the only man who mattered to her.

Margriet entered the house to find that visitors had arrived. Thorfinn and his men sat at her father's table, drinking ale…and waiting for her. Confused by Magnus's presence with them, she was just about to greet him when they stood and left, taking every servant with them. Then only she and Thorfinn remained and Margriet feared her penance had only just begun.

Rurik rode as though the devil was on his trail, when he knew that the devil he sought was already ahead of him. The message had been left while he'd been out seeing to his father's business and now Thorfinn and his men had a two-hour advantage over him. Sven, Donald and Leathen rode with him, silent, all remembering the servant girl's body and thinking of Margriet's fate if they did not reach her in time.

No one complained. No one slowed their pace or asked to stop. No one voiced the fear that ate at their guts as they rode. Finally as the sun reached its highest point in the sky, they reached the hills beyond which lay Gunnar's estates and Margriet.

With only a hand signal, they followed Rurik's orders, dismounted and followed him on foot, leaving the horses hobbled in the field. They crawled the final hundred or so yards so they would not be seen. The house was surrounded by more guards than they expected and they were seriously outnumbered.

While they hurriedly planned their attack, a scream rang out…one they each recognized from when she'd fallen in the river on their journey there. Any hope of surprising those on guard fell at the sound of her terror.

With swords and daggers drawn, Rurik screamed out his own cry and led the men to the house.

"I will not stand here and let you murder my child, Thorfinn."

Margriet wiped the blood that streamed down her face with the back of her hand and positioned herself now with her back to the wall. At least that way, she could see him coming at her.

He'd sent everyone out, except his man Sigurd, and then he'd tried to batter her down. She'd fought back, though not enough to keep him from bloody-

ing her nose and mouth and landing a powerful blow
on her back. He could have ended it much faster with
a blade or sword, but he seemed to enjoy delivering
the pain with his hands…and his feet. She'd dodged
two kicks aimed at the babe in her belly before blocking herself behind the long table.

"I did not ask you to, Margriet. Truly I like the
challenge of catching you before I beat it out of you."

"Holy Mother of God!" she cried, still not believing that he was so evil as to do that. "Why?" she
cried. "Why?"

When he grabbed hold of the table between them
and shoved it aside, she knew he was. She still brandished the leg of a chair he'd thrown at her as she ran
and hoped it would be strong enough to defend herself
with. Margriet swung it as he approached, but he waited
and grabbed it from her hands as it swung by him.

"I do not need that bastard at all and, now that your
dowry is in my coffers, I need you less."

She had no place to run now. He grabbed by the
hair and dragged her to him. He raised his fist, but
Magnus came running in. "Magnus! Help me!" she
screamed to him.

"My lord, he is here."

My lord? He called Thorfinn "lord" now? She
struggled in his arms, trying to tear herself from him
but she was lost against his superior strength.

"Sigurd, go and greet my brother," he ordered. "I
will finish here." The brute bowed then to Thorfinn
and left, heading, she knew, to kill Rurik.

"You will not get away with this, Thorfinn," she said. "The servants know. Someone will tell my father. Or yours."

He dragged her out away from the wall and tossed her on the floor. She tried to crawl to the door, but he feinted with kicks that kept her where he wanted her. "Did you not hear the warnings about the outlaws lately seen near the coast? They have been attacking some of the outlying cottages," he said with a smile. "I did warn your father to assign extra men, but he did not heed my warning."

He was about to make what she thought would be the killing attack, when Magnus stepped from the shadows and came up behind him. Thorfinn never saw the blow and fell in a crumpled heap at her feet.

"Come, lady. I must get you out of here," he said, reaching for her and trying to help her to her feet.

She found she could not stand on her own and it took several minutes before she stood. Just as he began guiding her to the door, Thorfinn came to and jumped up behind Magnus.

"I think not, Magnus," he said in deadly quiet as he plunged his dagger into the man's back.

Margriet watched in horror as Magnus sank to his knees before her, blood pouring from his wound onto the floor. "Forgive me, lady," he begged. With his last bit of strength, Magnus waited until Thorfinn grabbed his shoulders to shove him out of the way and plunged his own dagger into Thorfinn's chest. "Tell Rurik I served him at the last."

Both men fell back and Margriet stayed hunched down on the floor. The sounds of fighting outside reached her, but she could not move. Curling up on the floor, she could feel herself slipping away when she heard a bloodcurdling scream.

Rurik was here and she knew she was safe now.

He sent for Gunnar once they'd fought their way in and found Margriet unconscious on the floor. His heart stopped in that moment when he saw the two men and all the blood, but she murmured a sound as he picked her up to take her away from this. Within a day, Gunnar arrived, put his house back to rights and arranged for Margriet's care. Rurik discovered later that it had been her walk that saved her that day, for it was the delay he needed to catch up with Thorfinn.

And Magnus's actions, as Margariet had related them, and his decision to turn against Thorfinn in those last moments, had contributed to her rescue.

The story that Thorfinn planned to use to cover her murder worked well for his own demise and Erengisl promised the other landowners along the coast that he would add additional guards to protect them from such marauders. If he suspected or guessed the real cause, he never spoke of it. Although it galled him that Thorfinn should be thought of as a hero for trying to defend his betrothed against an attack, Rurik could accept it since he was dead and would not be a threat to her again.

He spoke of the future to no one and did not burden Margriet with questions or declarations, but he knew what he had to do. After a month had passed and the documents for his marriage contract arrived to be signed, he went to see his father.

"I wondered when this would happen."

"It has crossed my mind as well, Father."

He walked to the window and looked across to the harbor. Fewer boats and ships now as autumn was preparing to give way to winter. Soon, the sea would be completely inhospitable to travelers. His father approached holding out a cup of wine.

"I would accept your good wishes, Rurik."

"And I would give them, if I knew why." He waited for his father to reveal the cause, but his father paused and met his gaze for a minute before speaking of the cause for celebration.

"Agnes will bear a child in the spring."

Rurik smiled and held the cup up in a salute.

"I was not certain how you would take the news."

How far they'd come in the last seven months, for now his father worried over his reactions instead of the other way round. How far they still had to go, he thought.

"I am pleased for both of you. Agnes must be happy?"

"Aye. This is her first child and she is worrying already over the smallest things."

"There are many months to go and many more

things to worry on," he added. Now, with this news, mayhap his would not be so bad.

His father got the pitcher of wine and poured them both more. Sitting down again, Erengisl spoke first. "So, when do you leave?"

"How did you know?"

"I did not know, Rurik, I only suspected." His father drank deeply and then put the cup down. "You have dragged your feet on approving each one of the provisions for your marriage contract. You have not built the house you talked about in Birsay. You have not set up your own council yet. All signs of someone not yet convinced of his place here."

"I do not belong here, Father. In spite of your welcome and your offer, this is not my life."

"Has she agreed to marry you?"

He paused, surprised by his father's ability to discern what it had taken him months to realize. He'd done nothing in these months except mourn the missed opportunity to claim the woman he loved. It did not take him long to realize his mistake, but it was only recently that a solution was possible.

"I have not asked her yet. She will not see me."

"Do you blame her?" His father watched him closely as he asked that question and even more closely as he waited for an answer.

"Nay. 'Twas my mistake that drove her into his grasp. But, I will not give up until she has forgiven me my stupidity."

"So you will learn from your father's mistakes then?"

Rurik looked at the man he never thought to call father again and remembered the question he'd challenged him with on his arrival. A question about the things Erengisl had done in the past and the question of whether he'd made the correct decision. "Do you admit it was a mistake?"

His father laughed as he met question with question. He smiled then and nodded. "You asked if losing her was worth all I gained. My answer to you is that love lost or given up is never worth what you gain in its stead."

"Are you angry that I will upset all you put into place now?"

"Nay, Rurik. I am not that old yet and have many years yet to make arrangements. And with an heir on the way, there will be other sons to give my lands and wealth to." His father then grew serious. "So, when do you leave?"

"I have some arrangements to work out and a bride to ask and then I hope to be back in Lairig Dubh before the winter sets in." He could think of nothing he'd like more than spending the long, cold winter nights in his cottage, wrapped around Margriet. "If she'll have me."

His father stood and offered his hand. Rurik took hold of it and then pulled his father close.

"There will always be a place for you here, Rurik, if you decide you want to return."

His throat tightened with unshed tears so he simply nodded and walked away. Just as he reached the door, his father added a comment.

"I would appreciate it, man to man, if you did not tell your mother I admitted that she was right."

"Mother? Is she here?"

"Nay. But Margriet left for Scotland two weeks ago. Gunnar said she returned to the convent in Caithness."

"And Mother?" he asked, dreading the answer he knew would come. "Please tell me it is not so. Tell me she is not the person who has been raising Margriet for all these years."

His father cleared his throat and nodded. "She is known now to those at the convent as Reverend Mother Ingrid."

Chapter Twenty-Two

Convent of the Blessed Virgin
Caithness, Scotland

"If she does not come out in one hour, I will burn this convent to the ground and take her by force."

The sound of his threat rang hollow, but what else was he to do?

He'd arrived here three days ago and neither Margriet or his mother would speak to him. He pleaded, he begged, he promised, he bribed and still she would not speak to him about his offer of marriage. He was running out of time and options.

Sven snorted from behind him, reminding him that Elspeth had also taken refuge within the convent's walls with Margriet. And Sven was not happy. Rurik placed himself squarely in front of the gates and screamed her name out again.

Finally, the sound of whispering from above gained his attention. He moved back so he could see who stood there.

"Margriet," he said through clenched teeth. "I am trying to respect the sanctity of this convent, but you are making it difficult."

"I need more time," she said.

"The betrothal agreements have been signed by my father and yours, Margriet."

"But I have not given my consent, Rurik."

"Open the gates, so that we might discuss this privately."

"Do you swear not to force me from the convent?"

"Rurik!" Sven yelled. "Swear to anything, just get those damned gates open and get my wife!"

In spite of the hurried marriage after a nonexistent courtship, Sven had taken to married life like a pig in s…mud. Now, separated from Elspeth for these last three weeks, he was not in good humor. Surrendering to defeat, Rurik leaned his head against the gate and gave her the words she wanted.

"Yes, Margriet, I swear it. Now, *please* open the gates!"

He heard the bar lifted from the gates and stepped away as they swung open. He waited for Margriet to climb down from the tower and arrive there. Once there, he walked up to her and kissed her, as he'd been itching to do for all the months he could or dared not. And then he kissed her again. After the third time, Sven swept past him to claim his wife for the same kind of passionate reunion.

"Rurik?"

Another voice intruded into his wooing but he really did not want to stop for this one.

"Rurik?"

He lifted his mouth from hers only long enough to let her breathe and then he wrapped his arms around her and kissed her breathless again.

"Rurik!"

He stopped for a moment and answered the call now. If he knew his mother, and he did even though several years had passed since their last meeting, she would continue until she had his attention.

"'Tis the custom to gain the bride's consent before the next steps are taken."

"Yes, Mother," he answered, knowing it would do no good to argue at this point.

Rurik released Margriet, being careful not to let her fall. He looked at the woman he loved, the woman who was worth giving up everything he'd ever wanted in his life, for he'd gained more than he lost in loving her. Now, if she would only consent to marrying him, they could proceed with all the good parts.

"Margriet, would you do me the honor of becoming my wife?"

Although most of the trouble she'd put him through by fleeing back to the convent and using his mother as a guard were not really trouble at all, he did not want her to think this was not the most serious thing he'd done in his life.

"I know that I did not live up to your trust. And that I should have protected you against…" He hesitated to even speak the name. "But I promise that I will never…"

She reached up and covered his mouth with her hand then, stopping him from rattling on about his mistakes.

"Will you love me, Rurik?" she asked in a soft voice.

"I do love you."

"Will you trust me?"

"I do trust you, Margriet."

"Will you do all the things that Elspeth has told me about when we spend our long winter nights together?"

He lifted her from the ground and twirled around with her in his arms. "I will."

"Then I will marry you, Rurik."

The cheers began inside and soon, all the inhabitants of the convent—religious and lay alike—were offering their good wishes to the couple. Rurik heard a deeper voice behind him and turned to see a portly priest walking up to the gate. He frowned as the priest greeted him.

"I sent for Father as soon as we knew you were on your way," his mother said. "I knew that once you got hold of her, you would not let her go."

He had not, he realized as he looked down to where he held on to her hand, entwining their fingers together.

"With your reputation, I also knew you want the

consummation as soon as possible and that means a wedding first."

"Mother!" Rurik said, shocked at the way his mother understood his thinking.

But later, as he wrapped himself around his new wife and spent the night in her arms, he was glad his mother knew him enough to plan ahead.

He built a tent for her, one not too different from the one he built on their journey north, but with many layers of furs and woolen blankets for her comfort. The heat he would provide. Since men were not welcome in the convent overnight and since there was no way he would let Margriet out of his sight or grasp now that he had her to wife, he spent a good part of the day finding just the right location for their first night together as man and wife. The sisters did offer their version of a wedding feast and Rurik accepted it with all their good wishes. Now, Sven and Elspeth camped near the gates and he'd led Margriet deeper into the forest for privacy. Once there, he lifted the flap of the tent and helped her inside.

He knew she was uncomfortable with the shape and size of her body now that her pregnancy moved into its last months, but Rurik loved the way she blossomed with life. Any concerns about how he felt about her melted at his first touch. Margriet trusted him in this, too. And the reverend mother's advice, shocking though it was, eased any fears she had.

The last time he'd touched her had been in such

anger, but this time he slid his hands over her, gently removing her tunic and gown and even her chemise, until she lay naked in his arms. Somehow, and she did not remember how, his clothes disappeared and the touch of his skin to hers made her sigh.

Her breasts were heavier now and the nipples sensitive to his touch, and she watched as he drew circles around them with one finger and then he leaned his head down and kissed them. The ache grew deep within her and she pressed herself against him, wanting more.

Rurik drew in the tip of one breast and laved it with his tongue. Just as she felt the tension grow inside her, he moved to the other and continued there, moving back and forth, licking and sucking, until she slid her hand through his hair and held him there. He laughed and it was a wondrous sound to her.

He moved then so that he did not press too heavily on her, but lay at her side. He kissed her mouth in the way she liked it and Margriet felt her toes curl at the sensation he created in her. Their tongues touched and he suckled there as well, sending more waves of pleasure through her. His hand crept down to rest on the curls between her legs and she found it caused a different kind of feeling there. When she writhed against him, seeking more of his touch, he granted it, dipping one finger, then another into the moisture he'd caused there and drawing it out.

The tension within her built, ever tighter, ever stronger, as he created a new ache, a new need, a new pleasure with every touch. Margriet reached out to touch his hardness, hoping to give him some pleasure, too, but he shook his head.

"Nay, love, or your wedding night will be a short one."

"Let me touch you, Rurik," she said softly.

His eyes were filled with love as he relented and leaned away so she could touch him there. She had thought he would stop his attentions, but he did not and instead he returned every touch, every stroke with one of his own. "Margriet, stop now," he asked on a moan a few minutes later. She rested her hand there, and allowed him to continue to touch her as he had a mind to. Soon though she knew it would not last much longer, for his touches inflamed her, made her cry out for more.

"Come, love," he said, reaching for what used to be her waist and lifting her up. He guided her over him and when she slid down the hard length of him, his moans matched hers. Without delay, he slipped his hand between them and stroked her there, enticing even more wetness and aching.

Everything within her tightened then, every muscle contracted, and she felt the length of him deep within her as they reached the edge together and fell over it. He thrust deeper and deeper until she gasped and fell over on his chest. Wrapping his arms around her, he held her close for several minutes until their breaths came back.

The sounds of night surrounded them, but the

sound she loved the most was that of his heartbeat, strong and steady, against her ear as she rested against his chest. Margriet was nearly asleep when he spoke.

"And that is what happens when you surrender to a highlander."

She laughed as the thought of spending countless nights with him, paying his price, filled her thoughts. And she paid that price willingly several more times before the light of morning waked them to a new day.

Epilogue

The weather had turned colder much sooner than he'd planned, so their travel took more time. There was a threat of snow in the air as they rode up through the village to the Broch Dubh castle. Margriet sat on his lap, wrapped in the heavy woolen tartan and warmed by his body. She'd fallen asleep several miles back and he did not wish to wake her yet.

He watched her sleep and thanked God for bringing her to him. He watched her when she walked and talked and ate, and every time she did anything and marveled that she was—after so many trials—his alone. He watched her when she put her hand on the growing bairn and frowned and knew she worried about what was to come. Now he watched her as she came to wakefulness in his arms as they passed through the gate.

"You should have woken me, Rurik. I would not want to greet your laird like a bairn asleep in your arms."

"I liked you asleep like a bairn in my arms."

She straightened them and moved the plaid from her face so she could see the castle. He told her of it so much she probably knew each stone and each crevice of it. He'd never realized how much he missed living here until he did not, nor did he realize how much he missed the people of Lairig Dubh until he'd almost given them up. Now, he could see Connor standing high on the walls in his favorite place, with Jocelyn at his side.

He waved to several people as they passed, but did not stop, for he wanted her to meet the laird and his lady before anyone else there. When he reached the steps of the keep, he stopped and handed her down to one of the MacLerie soldiers standing guard. Taking her from him, he helped her to stand, giving her time to adjust after riding for so long.

By the time her legs steadied under her, Connor and Jocelyn came through the doors and walked down to greet them. With his plaid draped around her, it was hard to see more than the top of her head, but he could not wait for their reaction when they discovered the rest.

"Laird, lady," he said in formal greeting, "may I present you to my wife, Margriet Gunnarsdottir."

Jocelyn, soft-hearted as she was, burst into tears and pulled both Margriet and him to her in a hug that threatened to stop his breath. Then, when she felt the shape beneath the plaid, she simply screamed. Her embrace then, without Margriet between them, warmed his heart as no other woman could.

"You have been a busy man, Rurik Erengislsson," Connor teased as he held out his hand in greeting. "I thought you went to take her home, not bring her home."

They decided not to reveal the babe's origins to anyone else, so he held his tongue and let them believe what they wanted. He would be father to the child, so it mattered little to him how it all started out. Rurik would be the last one to love and care for Margriet and their child…and any more that God granted them.

Rurik laughed then, realizing that sometimes you had to move away to learn how important people and places were to you. Looking down at Margriet chattering happily now to Jocelyn and watching as Connor looked with love at his wife, he was surprised at how much you could give up to keep the most important thing in life.

* * * * *

On sale 7th August 2009

SCANDALOUS DECEPTION
by Rosemary Rogers

From the glittering ballrooms of London to the shimmering palaces of czarist Russia, *New York Times* bestselling sensation Rosemary Rogers returns with a sweeping tale of dangerous love and divided loyalties.

Desperate to escape her lecherous stepfather, flame-haired Brianna Quinn seeks refuge with the Duke of Huntley, a childhood friend. But her hopes crumble when she discovers that Edmond, the duke's hot-blooded twin, is masquerading as the duke to thwart an assassination scheme…

With nowhere to turn, Brianna plays into the intrigue as Edmond's fiancée – and soon their forced proximity ignites into a burning desire. But when Edmond's enemies threaten Brianna, he must choose between his countrymen and the woman he loves more than life itself…

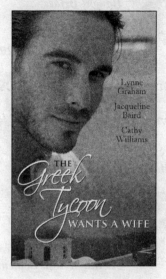

2 FREE

BOOKS AND A SURPRISE GIFT!

We would like to take this opportunity to thank you for reading this Mills & Boon® book by offering you the chance to take TWO more specially selected titles from the Historical series absolutely FREE! We're also making this offer to introduce you to the benefits of the Mills & Boon® Book Club™—

- ★ FREE home delivery
- ★ FREE gifts and competitions
- ★ FREE monthly Newsletter
- ★ Exclusive Mills & Boon Book Club offers
- ★ Books available before they're in the shops

Accepting these FREE books and gift places you under no obligation to buy, you may cancel at any time, even after receiving your free shipment. Simply complete your details below and return the entire page to the address below. You don't even need a stamp!

YES! Please send me 2 free Historical books and a surprise gift. I understand that unless you hear from me, I will receive 4 superb new titles every month for just £3.79 each, postage and packing free. I am under no obligation to purchase any books and may cancel my subscription at any time. The free books and gift will be mine to keep in any case.

H9ZED

Ms/Mrs/Miss/Mr ....Initials ....

BLOCK CAPITALS PLEASE

Surname ....

Address ....

....

....Postcode..................................

Send this whole page to:
UK: FREEPOST CN81, Croydon, CR9 3WZ